RODEO SNOW

PAT RHOADES

To Rachel —
Carry It Forward !
Love,
Pat

NORTH STAR PRESS OF ST. CLOUD, INC.
St. Cloud, Minnesota

Cover design: Brad Kaspari
Kaspari Design Services, Inc.
www.kasparidesign.com

ISBN: 978-0-87839-731-0

First Edition: June 2014

Printed in the United States of America

Published by
North Star Press of St. Cloud, Inc.
P.O. Box 451
St. Cloud, MN 56302

northstarpress.com

For
my parents, Ron and Jeanette Rhoades
and for
my children, James and Rachel Kaspari

CHAPTER ONE

ROAD RAGE

You're merging onto the freeway for the second time in your life. Only this time instead of just your dad riding shotgun, the whole family's there: mom, sister, Yellow, the dumb dog who worships you. The whole family's buckled their fate into yours, depending on you not to blow it. So you do all the stuff they bored you with in driver's ed: signal, look in the rearview mirror, double check over your shoulder, try to get up the guts to floor it when suddenly there's this big pig SUV from nowhere on your butt honking, then pulling up alongside you, the guy giving you the finger and edging closer trying to run you off the road. What do you do?

A. Give him the finger back and yell, "Screw you, mister!" For once your mother will have to make an exception to her rule against bad language.
B. Ask your dad to get the gun (which, by the way, doesn't exist) from the glove compartment.
C. Pull off the road, vowing to limit all future driving to pulling the car into the garage.
D. Keep on the road the best you can, telling yourself this asshole, like all bad things, will pass.

Since no gun was available, I thought C was the best option, but my dad said, "Hold it steady, son. It'll be okay," and the guy blasted past us.

"Can I pull over?" I asked. "I can't do this."

Dad said, "You did great, Gene. If you stop driving just because of all the jerks on the road, you'll have to skate everywhere."

But that's exactly what I wanted to do. I was a skater. Aggressive inline, as in rollerblades. A street skater. I was no skateboarding wood pusher. When I was wearing my skates I could get away from anyone.

"You almost got us killed!"

"Shut up, Lily." I glared at my sister in the rearview mirror.

"Shhh!" Mom said. "Gene's a good driver. He isn't the one trying to run people off the road."

I stayed in the slow lane the rest of the way and finally pulled into the parking lot. "I don't think I can drive home."

"Of course you can," Mom insisted. It probably took a lot of effort for her to encourage me. But encouragement was Mom's deal. She was a kindergarten teacher whose classroom motto was from that ancient little kid's book: *The Little Engine Who Could*. You know, you do what seems impossible because you tell yourself, "I think I can, I think I can."

It was our monthly trip to the Cud, that's what our family called the Ruminator Bookstore. The store's symbol was a wood cut of a cow chewing its cud or, as they say in Honors English, ruminating. It used to be called The Hungry Mind, but they sold their name to someone on the Internet. Dad said that's what you had to do to survive in the year 2002: pretend you'd sold your soul so the buyer thought what they got was worth something.

I wished I could sell my name. Hell, I wouldn't have charged much. But who would've bought it? I mean how many kids do you know named Eugene? Most of the time when I told kids my name they looked confused and said "Jean?" like my parents got mixed up and thought I was a girl or "U-Gene?" like I was some kind of biological experiment.

When I told them I was named after Eugene McCarthy, the peacenik politician, they said something ignorant like, "Isn't he the guy who hated Communists?" That guy's name was Joe, a name I wouldn't have minded at all. In fact that's what I looked like: brown hair, generically okay face, almost medium height. An ordinary Joe. But I could guarantee my parents would've never named me after a Republican.

Dad told me once if it had been up to him, he would've named me after his favorite musician.

"Captain Beefheart?" I wondered.

He shook his head.

"Frank?" I still would've been stuck with a geezer name.

"Zappa." He grinned.

"Zappa." I found myself smiling every time I thought of it. Frank Zappa was this totally weird rock dude with this album called *Weasels Rip My Flesh*. He named his kids, I kid you not, Moon Unit and Dweezil.

So I was obsessed with names. When we got our dog, Yellow, a couple of winters before, Lily watched him pee in the yard. "Eeeww, yellow snow!" she said and I'm sorry to say that since he was a yellow lab, I went for it. After all, Snow is our last name. Of course he was such a dumb, trusting mutt he came the first time I called him.

We started going to the Ruminator each month to buy books with the money my parents saved by canceling cable. I didn't mind—I just went over to my friend Andy's house to watch *Adult Swim* and, if I didn't leave it to my mom, I usually got something decent to read out of the arrangement. That day I was looking for a skate magazine. I was doing everything I could to get ready for the street skate competition that fall: studying videos, poring over skate mags. Oh, and of course, skating. I spent the summer in my skates.

I figured that if I could win the fall comp, win some bucks from the communal pot, and establish myself, I could go on to win the big company-sponsored comp in the spring. Winning a company competition got you hooked up with free skates and skate clothes, a chance to do demos, maybe even get some tricks on an amateur mixed tape. It was the only way to get treated seriously as a skater.

"I found a book for you." Mom walked over just as I located a mag with this crazy cover shot: Chris Edwards, the first and best street skater of all time, suspended over a never-ending staircase. No wonder they called him the Airman. Mom waved her book in front of me, bringing me back to earth. I groaned as I realized it was another one of her attempts to indoctrinate me: *The Conscience of a Liberal* by Paul Wellstone.

"Mom, it's the end of summer vacation. Have pity on me."

"It's not a punishment, Gene," she said.

"Mom, I'll probably read it in school anyway."

"Do you think so?" I could see she was distracted by her fantasy of the whole high school studying her favorite politician, our senator who was running for his third term in office. If we all read this book, we teenagers could save the world.

I turned back to my mag. There was an article on Louie Zamora. The dude was like a human superball bouncing off any surface in sight. He was one crazy skater.

"Gene," Mom continued, but I didn't look at her. I just walked to the cash register where Lily and Dad were standing. Dad, the self-employed artist had his usual coffee table art book. Lily, typical eight-year-old, held the latest Harry Potter. Even though she'd read my copy, she had to have her own in hardcover.

"Gene." Mom followed me.

"It's not fair," I told her. "Last time you got me the PSAT study guide." Mom was all worried about my studying for the PSAT even though it was just a practice test for the SAT. You'd think she would've realized I didn't need to practice my test taking skills. That's all we did in school.

"You didn't come with us last time," she reminded me.

"I'm here now," I reminded her.

She still had the Paul Wellstone book when we checked out. "It's a gift," she explained, handing it to me.

I took it just to get her to leave me alone. Like she really thought I'd read it. It looked like the most boring book on the planet. Paul Wellstone smiled from the back cover like he expected something from me. I hid him under my skate mag. Chris Edwards wasn't smiling. He was flying.

I drove home at what felt like a hundred miles per hour (okay, actually sixty-five) and I was still getting passed by assholes. At least I finally made it, so I could call Andy on my cell and have him meet me at the Stairs to practice. I put on my Shima 3's, the inline skates I saved up for and finally bought at the beginning of the summer. The figure skating white had already faded to an urban gray, except for the sides where I'd lettered the word *soul*, with blue and black paint markers, graffiti style. Soul: as in soul grind, soul slide, blindside halfcab soul, oversoul—if you skate you gotta have soul. And I was out the door, the wheels pushing me up to my desired height, like bionic feet helping me move faster and more freely than any car, jock or wild animal.

The Stairs were the front entrance to St. Joan's Parish House, a convent where a bunch of ancient nuns lived, a couple of blocks from my house. It was Andy's and my usual meeting place and the gathering place for all the skaters in the neighborhood.

I couldn't imagine living in some suburban cul de sac with no sidewalks where all the kids wore helmets and kneepads and got their parents to dish out the bucks for them to go to indoor skate parks whenever they wanted. When I was skating down the sidewalk to the Stairs, I was who I was born to be: a Minneapolis street skater.

I put on speed once I approached the Stairs, skated up the ramp, then ground the concrete ledge alongside it. Grinding is when you jump onto an edge or rail and slide sideways down it on your skates. Pretty basic but the variations are endless. No Andy yet and the Stairs were deserted, so I royaled the steps, another grind. I slid down the ledge on the side of one foot, dragging the other behind for emphasis. Kind of an inline underline.

Then I started messing with what would have been a blindside halfcab soul if I could've done it right. What you do is skate backwards at the rail or ledge you're going to grind, then do a 180 to soul, the lengthwise outer edge of your skates, spinning so you lose sight of the rail. The backwards part was no big deal, but most of the time when I turned away from the edge I missed it. As a result, I had some pretty intense bruises.

Of course it hurt to get good at an extreme sport like skating. My legs looked like a bad painting of a sunset. It was great how freaked out girls got when they saw me in shorts. It made my mom semi-hysterical.

I wiped out as usual, and as I got up I thought I heard Andy. "You're late, asshole," I started to complain but then I saw it wasn't him. It was a girl on skates. Cute, but maybe she should have stayed on the sidewalk with the baby strollers. She paused at the Stairs. I skated backwards casually a ways so I could watch. Of course, instead of doing some dumb move badly she nailed a blindside half cab soul. Damn, she must have been watching—and laughing at me.

"Wow," Andy skated up on his board just in time to witness my humiliation. "Who are you?" he asked and I could see he was smitten.

"Core-in," she said, emphasizing the "in." "C-o-r-i-n-n-e," she spelled when we looked confused. She was good looking in a tough way: heavy on the eye makeup, baggy cargo pants and tight little top that didn't cover much. I caught the glint of a nose ring as she turned her head and pulled her dark gold hair back into a ponytail.

"Nice skates." She glanced at me. I wondered if she was implying that my skates were too good for me because it wasn't like she said nice skat*ing*.

Possible insults and tough girl answers didn't stop Andy though. Nothing stopped Andy. He kind of reminded me of Yellow that way: my two obnoxiously eager best friends. Andy was tall and skinny and sort of loped around, bouncing his head up and down like he was both sheepish and happy to be there. His hair, which was golden-retriever brown and shaggy, hung in his face, goofy and dog-like.

But as Mom always said, looks can be deceiving: Andrew Carter Carlson, Junior, had the most diabolically intelligent creative mind of anyone I knew. He got straight A's and invented these amazingly bizarre devices—the electronic younger sibling zapper guaranteed to deter your little brother or sister from snooping in your room (although if your mother got zapped, you were in deep crap), the ultra-sanitary garbage catapult, which sent a bag of garbage sailing over your garage into the alley where you could easily pop it into the bin with a minimum of stinky garbage bag contact.

The guy was a good-natured evil genius. He grinned and skated up to Corinne, introducing himself, "I'm Andy and this is—" he turned to me.

"Gene," I finished. Don't ask, I thought, bracing myself for the usual what the hell kind of name is that question. But she just nodded and shrugged simultaneously, like acknowledging our existence bored her.

We took turns on the Stairs. I decided not to do anything too ambitious, instead I stayed simple and successful. Andy, who was a skate boarder, was out of the competition and did what he wanted. Corinne did all these crazy jumps and twists. The way she skated reminded me of someone, but I wasn't sure who.

"Anywhere good to skate around here?"

I felt a bit defensive about the question like the Stairs weren't good enough, which I realized was true but they were good enough if you needed something close by. "There's Nollie Ollie at the U," I said, "but it's kind of far."

"Nollie Ollie? U?" She was finally interested enough to have an extended conversation. She stopped and looked at me. Smiled. It was a smile in need of orthodontia but in a crookedly attractive way.

Andy nosed in like a puppy dog. "It's a concrete plaza at the University of Minnesota." He did an ollie, popping his board up under one foot. Then he did a nollie popping it up under the other. She really smiled at that. "It's a pretty random name," he admitted, looking pleased with himself. "Next time we go, we'll take you there."

"Do you guys have a car?"

"Well, no," Andy admitted.

"License?" She sounded hopeful.

"Permit," I said.

"I can take my test at the end of the school year," Andy said.

She looked at me like I should come up with something better, like I was turning sixteen the next week.

"March," I said.

"How about you?" I asked, wondering why we were acting like getting a driver's license was a male prerogative.

"I haven't had a chance to take driver's ed yet," she admitted.

"What grade are you?"

"I'll be a sophomore," she said.

"Hey, us too." Andy was falling head over heels for this girl. Like he'd really have had a chance with her. A skater would have been more her type. A really good skater. Like the winner of the skate comp. Like, well, like me.

"My mom and I just moved here from Barrington. Chicago," she explained. No wonder she was so good. She was a street skater from a real city. "Now I'm registered at this loser school."

"Too bad," I commiserated.

"South High." She wrinkled up her nose like it was the home of the Turds not the Tigers.

"Hey, that's our loser school," Andy said happily, like he could imagine the two of them sharing a romantic moment in Algebra II.

"You could always transfer," I suggested. It seemed like a lot of work to get this girl to like us. I wasn't sure I wanted to spend the school year with her looking down her nose ring at us.

"That's creepy," Andy interrupted. He pointed to the giant wood door at the top of the Stairs. It creaked open. We stood staring as a big silver-haired woman in a ratty black tunic and a skirt that was so faded the flowers on it look dead, walked out. She looked us up and down and lit a cigarette.

"You can leave now," she said. Andy had this expression on his face like we'd entered the Twilight Zone. I didn't know who this Goth bag lady was. All I knew was that the old nuns who lived there wouldn't have been able to push that door open even if they'd all pushed together. They used the side door and never said boo to us.

Andy and I turned to leave, but Corinne said, "Excuse me? We were here first."

The woman sat down, raised her bushy eyebrows, took a drag off her cigarette and exhaled. "Excuse me, honey," she said, "but God was here first."

"God?" Corinne said like maybe she'd heard her wrong.

"This is a house of God. There are enough hungry people out there that God doesn't want me wasting his money repairing steps wrecked by roller skaters." The woman didn't take her unblinking owl eyes off Corinne.

"Roller skaters?" Corinne was outraged. "Look lady," Corinne raised her voice. "We're not wrecking anything. Churches, or whatever this place is, are public places and we have just as much right to be here as anybody." She turned to Andy and me. "Right?"

Andy shrugged. I started to both halfheartedly agree and disagree but it was clear Andy and I weren't really part of the conversation.

"What you're doing is called loitering and damaging church property. You don't have any right to be here at all." The lady stood up and walked down until she was on the same step as Corinne. Even though she was barefoot and Corinne had on roller blades, she towered over her. "Honey, in my old neighborhood this would be called gang activity."

Corinne laughed. "You think these Boy Scouts are gang members?"

The woman raised her eyebrows again. "You're right," she said. "You're just a bunch of spoiled middle-class kids who think you're entitled to everything. I should call the cops on you."

"You've got a lot of nerve calling me spoiled," Corinne raised her voice. "I'm not like them," she said, giving us a look of disgust like we were Ambercrombie and Fitch models or something. "I'm practicing for the skate competition."

The skate comp? My stomach sank. And all of a sudden it came to me. She reminded me of Louie Zamora. She skated that good and crazy.

"You want me to call the cops, I'll call the cops," the woman threatened. Andy and I backed away as the two of them started really yelling.

"Road rage," I said to Andy. "Let's leave before the cops show up." I felt like an asshole ditching this girl, but she'd brought it on herself. She could get herself in so much trouble she wouldn't be able to practice anywhere. Not me. I was gonna practice and win. Then she'd give me some respect. Then she'd show some interest—not that I'd reciprocate.

Andy looked reluctant. It was a good show and it starred his pseudo girlfriend. He finally nodded. "Time to accelerate," I said and rolled into motion, not realizing until I was almost home that Andy wasn't behind me.

11

CHAPTER TWO

CONCRETE HEAVEN

"Did she get arrested?" I asked Andy the next day. Mom had dropped us off at Nollie Ollie. *I know you like her,* I wanted to say, *but do you really think you'd have a chance? You're not even that good of a skater.*

"The police never came," Andy said. "They just yelled at each other some more."

"And?"

But Andy just smiled.

"Boy Scouts! Can you believe she called us Boy Scouts?" I figured Corinne had pretty well ruined the Stairs for us. It was guaranteed that lady'd be sitting there, chain-smoking, waiting.

I gave up trying to talk to Andy and started skating. I didn't like to waste time at a great place like Nollie Ollie. Skaters from all over the city came there and college students too.

That day I was working on my tweaked flat spin, which involved lots of concentration and maybe some blood. I started at the top of this immense concrete staircase, wiping out over and over again as I worked on spinning with my body horizontal. I was trying to be a human frisbee whizzing through the air, but I felt more like a human yo-yo. Finally I nailed it.

"Check this out." Andy skated up to me. I tried to tell him about my miraculous bloodless trick, but he wasn't paying attention. A group of guys—they looked college age—were at the big concrete ledge with a video camera. Andy and I watched as they shot this guy skating the ledge at I swear 100 miles an hour doing a back flip and spinning. A suicidal move. No wonder they call it a brainless.

The guy turned toward us, grinned and skated over. "You from this place?"

"Who us?" Andy couldn't believe this incredible skater would talk to us well, let's face it, Boy Scouts.

"Yeah, we're from here," I interrupted.

"This is so great, dudes." He acted like we were responsible for Nollie Ollie. He pulled off the blue bandana tied around his head to keep the sweat out of his eyes and I noticed the thing was wet, saturated. "I'm from Milwaukee. We don't have anything like this." He went on, "It's like concrete heaven."

He took us over and introduced us to the rest of his group. His name, it figured, was Joe and I felt a little nervous when he turned to me and told the three other guys, "This is Snow." He paused and wrinkled his forehead, trying to remember my first name.

"Gene." I barely croaked it out.

But Joe talked over me. "*Rodeo* Snow. Did you see him over there a few minutes ago? Dude, he rode those stairs like a bucking bronco."

Talk about heaven. I couldn't help but grin and wondered if I could convince my parents to let me legally change my name and start the new and improved version of my life. Rodeo Snow, a totally cool name. Almost as cool as Airman.

"Hey, Rodeo," Joe said. "Want to be in our video?"

"Sure," I shrugged. Inside I was alternating between jumping up and down with joy and being paralyzed with terror.

"How about you, Andy?"

"No thanks," he said. "I'm not really good enough. But Gene—I mean Rodeo—is." I could tell he was worried he'd blow this for me. "I am pretty good at making videos," he added.

"Cool," Joe said. "Technical assistance?"

"Sure." Andy shrugged like me. But I knew when we were alone he'd be doing his happy dog dance.

Technical assistance was what Andy did best. It was like he visualized this video all along and finally had the world's greatest skaters (or at least some really good ones) to act out his intensely dangerous fantasies.

I tried to repeat my flat spin on film, but instead wiped out more and more dramatically. My legs were starting to resemble raw hamburger. I started to apologize, but Joe stopped me.

"This is great stuff. C'mere and see this." So we all crowded around his digital video display. There I was wiping out over and over again in miniature. Everyone groaned in unison at each fall.

"We have to use this in our bail section," Joe said. "Don't worry, dude." He saw the discouraged look on my face. "There's a lot of footage of me there too. And you've got great skates."

Later, on our way to meet my mom, Andy said, "You'll still have a chance to get your flat spin down for posterity. We'll make an even better video."

I sighed. We'd been shooting all summer. Andy did the camera work. I downloaded background music and did the editing. So far we'd mostly filmed Andy's inventions in action and a few skate tricks. Mom offered to throw us an end-of-summer video premiere. What we had so far was pretty good.

When Mom picked us up, she announced that next Saturday was State Fair night. Every year right before Labor Day, our family went to the Great American Pig Out, which was what I called the Minnesota State Fair.

"Can Andy come with us?" I could tell Andy was in the back, his whole face a silent whine, *please, please.*

Mom got a glimpse of him in the rearview mirror and laughed. "Yes, Andy can come. How could I refuse a face like that?"

Okay, so I went out of my way to get Andy a ride to the fair and what did he do on Saturday but show up with that girl from the planet Turd, the girl of his dreams and my nightmares, Corinne.

"I hope it's okay I brought Corinne, Mrs. Snow," he said, like it just occurred to him to ask her permission. Of course, it never occurred to him to ask me. I should have stayed at the Stairs that day. If I'd stayed at the Stairs maybe Corinne would have gone with me, not Andy.

"I'm from Chicago, I've never been to the state fair," Corinne said, like she was this sweet innocent thing.

I've never been to the state fair. I made a prissy face and mimicked silently. Only Lily saw me and giggled.

Mom, however, was in full kindergarten mode and was thinking of this as a field trip. "You boys have to take her to the butter heads. They carve the heads of the dairy princesses out of big blocks of butter, " she tried to explain to Corinne, who nodded politely.

"And the crop art," Dad added. "You can't miss the pictures of Elvis in seeds." He was doing that thing he did, being sarcastic and sincere at the same time. Corinne looked really weirded out. Great, this experience was going to be further proof that we lived in Hicksville, USA.

We got into our ancient beige Volvo station wagon, which I'd never realized was a loser car until I saw Corinne wrinkle her nose at it. Thankfully, my dad didn't ask me to drive, but I had to figure out fast: should I sit in the middle seat, painfully sticking out, like a wart on the butt of love, or should I go to the very back with Lily, acknowledging that socially I was still in grade school?

I opted for the back. I didn't want Andy to have fantasies of attacking me with a giant bottle of Compound W. But instead of Lily, Corinne hopped in beside me.

"I've always wanted to ride facing the back," she said.

I was feeling pretty okay about being the third party of what didn't seem like much of a twosome, until we got there. Dad bought our family tickets to get in. Then Andy bought tickets for himself and Corinne. Great. The evidence was clear. This was a date.

"My parents said I have to spend time with my family," I said, as I crossed the turnstile. Mom looked at me in surprise. "Maybe I can catch up with you later," I added before she said something embarrassing like, "You just run along with your friends, Gene."

Andy seemed grateful. Like I had made up for what, I would like to point out, was not really my fault with the seating arrangements.

Corinne looked impressed at the river of people we just joined. The air was shimmering with heat and grease and the crowd seemed to be carried away in it.

"Meet us at the skate village," Andy said.

"Okay," I said. "I'll be there in an hour."

"Hour and a half," Andy blurted out, then blushed.

"Andy's got a girlfriend," Lily sang out, once we were far enough away that he couldn't hear. "And she has a disgusting nose ring. Ick!" she added.

"She seems like a nice kid. You shouldn't judge a person by their piercings," Mom said. But then Mom had never met a kid she didn't like or one she thought she couldn't save.

"You know, I was considering getting my nose pierced or maybe my eyebrow. What do you think?" Dad asked. He was the most boringly ordinary looking person I knew. Sometimes people had a hard time believing he was really an artist. If you asked me, he liked it that way.

"I think you should get your tongue pierced or maybe your bellybutton." Lily was so into this she walked right past the place where she usually begged for cotton candy.

"How about a beret or maybe a beanie," Mom said. "Less painful and easily removed for family photographs."

"Hey, what about my cotton candy?"

"A beanie?" Dad said. "You think I should wear a beanie?"

We walked around doing our share of pigging out. We stopped to get root beer from the stand that looked like a root beer barrel, and Dad said as usual, "I think it tastes better coming from a barrel, don't you?"

Then as she was eating a footlong, Lily freaked out like she did every year because she forgot to measure it with her free yardstick.

"You can buy another hot dog later," Mom tried to console her.

"I can't. I'm too full!" Lily wailed. But, of course, this didn't stop her from eating more than half of the mini donuts from the bag we were sharing.

"They're no good when they're cold," she said, repeating a line she'd heard from me.

"One of these years I'm going to apply for a job making mini donuts just so I can get one of those tee shirts." Mom looked back at the Tom Thumb Lite as Feather Mini Donut stand. Every year she admired the worker's shirts that had Tom Thumb riding his feather on the front of them.

"You couldn't wear it afterwards," Dad advised, like he'd never said this before. "It would be covered with grease stains."

I sighed. My family was so predictable that I could've written the script for our whole night there.

"Let's go to the pig barn," I suggested. My favorite thing was the biggest boar in Minnesota. It was a grunting mega monster, lying on its side while everyone stood around its pen, gaping at it.

"We're really close to Paul Wellstone's booth," Mom said. "Let's see if he's there."

"I should really find Andy and Corinne," I said. I had successfully avoided this guy in the past when my family made their annual pilgrimage. I tended to think of their political stuff as this embarrassing family religion: some people's parents were Jesus Freaks, some were Hare Krishnas. My parents worshipped certain Democrats.

Dad looked at his watch. "You've got plenty of time."

We walked about a block and there was the booth with the green-and-white Wellstone signs. Of course it was my bad luck he was actually there talking to a couple of people.

"Looks like there's a lull." Mom had this idea that everyone, every single person among the thousands at the state fair wanted to talk to Paul Wellstone and we just happened to be there when the line didn't snake through the Midway around the entire fairgrounds.

"Probably everyone around here is a Republican." Dad glanced around at all the weird people with T-shirts that read things like BEAM ME UP, SCOTTIE and AMERICA, HOME OF THE BUD.

"They are not!" said Mom, who always liked to think the best of people.

Lily, who had a lot of nerve, walked right up to Paul Wellstone as the other people left. "I drew this for you." She handed him a picture she pulled from her backpack.

He held it up, and we gathered around him to look at it. It was a school bus colored green with magic marker with the words GET ON THE BUS, GUS written in Lily's best printing above it. It was, of course, a drawing of the Wellstone campaign bus, this cool old painted school bus he rode around in when he was running for election. Paul Wellstone went nuts when he saw this. He beamed and hugged Lily, shook her hand and thanked her again and again. He told her she should join his campaign staff. He could put her in charge of lawn signs. She beamed at him and it occurred to me that this guy really liked kids. He got one of his volunteers to find some tape and directed him to tape it up right at the top of his booth in the most prominent place.

"I'd do it myself," he told Lily. "But I'd have to find a chair to stand on." He would've needed a chair. This guy, who was our big deal senator from Minnesota, was one short dude. As I was considering his height, he turned to me and shook my hand. I about died of embarrassment. But of course, things could always get worse and did.

Mom said, "Gene's reading your book."

"You are!"

"He is."

"You are!" Of course he was totally thrilled by this. I found myself nodding.

So, you've just been caught in a lie, in an ultra fib by this really nice guy whose feelings you don't want to hurt by admitting you haven't read his book. Actually you'd rather plunge off the bungee cord tower to your death

than read his boring book. On top of that, he's a senator and knows the president of the United States, although you've heard they don't get along so well. So he's not just nice, he's important. What do you do?

A. Smile and pretend you read it, saying, "It was really interesting."
B. Visualize all the grease soaked cheese curds, pronto pups, and mini donuts you've already eaten until you turn green. Then say, "Excuse me, I don't feel well. " (This will not be a lie).
C. Say, "Yes and speaking of books have you read any good ones lately?"
D. Realize that this guy is a politician on the order of Honest Abe and George Washington, so you tell him, "I cannot tell a lie."

I, of course, took the idiot's way out and chose all four. Feeling the grease bubble up in my stomach, I said, "It looks really interesting . . . speaking of interesting books." He looked at me like he was really paying attention and it occurred to me not so much that he was really important but that he liked kids, so I blurted out, "but I haven't had a chance to read it yet."

"Of course not," he said. "It is summer vacation."

"Yeah," I agreed. Then he asked me about school and what sports I liked and I felt this huge gratitude towards him for helping me not look like a total loser.

"I hope you win," I said, just to be polite. "Thanks for questioning President Bush's Iraq policy," I added, wanting to redeem myself. To show that I, at least, listened to my parent's conversations at the dinner table.

He got all excited again. Kind of like Yellow when it was time to go for a walk. He put his arm around me, and we took a few steps away from everyone. It felt like my family, all the people who had started to line up behind us, the thousands of people milling around eating corn dogs had faded away, leaving just the two of us.

"Gene," he said, looking really happy and really serious at the same time. "I want your opinion. I'm trying to figure out which way to vote. There's a lot of pressure on me to vote for Bush's policy, but it may be the wrong thing to do. If I don't support Bush gearing up to go to war in Iraq, it could cost me the election—the election and all the good I could do."

"I wouldn't vote for you if you if you supported going to war with Iraq—that would be bullshit," I blurted out, turning red when I realized what I'd just said to a United States senator.

"Really!" He bounced up and down in excitement. "Gene—I want your vote."

"But I'm not old enough to vote."

"I represent you," he insisted. "I represent you just as much as I represent people who are old enough to vote. And I can't justify putting kids who are just a little older than you—Minnesota kids—in harm's way unless it's absolutely necessary." He gave me this expectant look like the way he looked on his book cover. "Thanks Gene, you've been a big help to me."

"Gene, stop hogging Paul Wellstone," Lily's whiney little voice cut in, bringing me back to the fair and the crowd of people around us.

Paul Wellstone laughed and reached out to shake the hand of the guy standing behind me.

"Say, Gene," he said, as I turned to leave. "Read my book when you get the chance. Next time I see you, I'll autograph it."

"Sure," I said, wondering how my dumb, barely-informed opinion could possibly help him.

"What were you two talking about?" Mom asked as we walked away.

"Nothing," I said. What should I have told her? That I was giving Paul Wellstone advice on foreign policy?

"Nothing?" She sounded disappointed that I was giving her my usual answer to her never-ending questions.

I took off to find Andy and Corinne, who I hoped weren't being too disgustingly friendly with each other. The skate park was close to the Midway. They had some good skaters and they had built this awesome set of ramps. Someday I planned to skate there, maybe next year after I won the spring comp. I found Andy and Corinne on a bench watching skate demos. They were sitting close together but at least they weren't holding hands.

"This is so tight," Andy told me. "Wait until you see this."

The guy at the microphone announced that it was time for their hourly give away. "This deck goes to the first person who can name three people who started the Bones Company."

Of course, Andy's hand shot up before I could even think to myself, *huh, who would know that?* The guy had him step up to the microphone. Corinne looked nervous, and I wanted to tell her not to bother. The guy was a walking encyclopedia.

He, of course, rattled off the names.

"You're right!" The announcer handed him the skateboard. Everybody clapped. Corinne and I both whistled. Andy shuffled back to his seat with the board under his arm, grinning.

"This is a good deck," he said.

Corinne and I admired it. "How'd you know the answer to that question?" she asked. "It was like so obscure."

I almost said he knew it because Andy knew everything but then I remembered she thought she knew everything herself and needed to be taken down a notch or two. "Because he goes to South High," I told her. "Maybe if you're there a few years, you'll catch up."

"Asshole," she said.

"Hey," Andy stepped in. "No fighting." Andy barely noticed how Corinne and I were trying to decide whether we merely disliked or truly hated each other. He was floating above it all in some kind of puppy-love heaven.

We walked around, stopped at a few food stands. Then we headed to the dairy barn to see the butter sculptures, the heads of Princess Kay of the Milky Way and her court carved out of big blocks of butter. Every year I was amazed at how these butter heads all looked alike, except for the length of their hair. None of them looked like the black-and-white photos next to them.

"I don't get it," Corinne complained. "Are they supposed to be funny or just weird?" We watched the giant yellow heads slowly turn on the glass enclosed carousel, kind of like an enormous pie display.

"I don't know," I said, thinking if you're going to criticize the state fair you shouldn't be allowed to come. "It's kind of like a nose ring," I said. "Is it supposed to be funny or just weird?"

She scowled at me. "I didn't say I didn't like them. I just don't know if you're supposed to take all this stuff seriously. It's so hokey,but everyone acts like it's so important. If my nose ring offends you, why don't you just say so?"

"I like your nose ring," Andy said. "Gene's just jealous."

"I am," I admitted, but I wasn't quite sure what I was jealous of.

We made our way back to the Midway, which was all lit up in the dark by then. Andy handed me his deck when he stopped to tie his shoe. He didn't take it back when he was done. Instead he held Corinne's hand.

"Let's go on the Ferris wheel," Corinne said. "I love the Ferris wheel."

When we finally got to the front of the line, the attendant said to me, "Sorry, you can't take that on the ride," pointing at Andy's skateboard. Corinne and Andy had already slid into the long seat. The guy locked the bar in place over their laps and moved the wheel to the next opening.

"Hey!" Andy and Corinne said in surprise.

"It's okay," I yelled to them, then squeezed my way out.

I found a bench nearby where I put the board down so nobody would sit next to me. I could hear all of the music from the different Midway rides clashing like a radio tuned between stations. The heat from the day rose from the asphalt and the air smelled like garbage. About a thousand colored lights were flashing and they were giving me a headache.

I remembered what it was like at the top of the Ferris wheel. Lily and I rode it every summer. I looked up and I was glad it was so high and far away that I couldn't see the riders. I couldn't see Andy and Corinne, as they gently swung back and forth in the seat at the top, in the cool breeze, up above all the noise. Where everything they looked down on seemed magical, lit up, and happy, all of the rest of us like ants in the distance.

CHAPTER THREE

POOP IN A BLENDER

"Showtime," Andy announced, as my friends elbowed each other to get the best seat in front of the computer. "You are offensive," Sam complained to Brady, moving off the couch they were sharing. You couldn't get two people much different than Sam, this tall, rich, mixed kid who wore FUBU and reeked of cologne, and Brady, this runty white boy with big hair, who we called Man Food, the Spanish translation for bo, B.O., body odor.

The music started. A little muffled, nothing investing in surround sound wouldn't have taken care of. I was feeling this combination of satisfaction and high anxiety as I tried to simultaneously watch their faces and the image of Sam, skating the Stairs to Sly and the Family Stone singing "Hot Fun in the Summertime." I knew the editing worked, but I still held my breath as Sam hovered over the Stairs in slow motion while Sly slo mo'd the chorus. It was perfectly synchronized, and I could tell everybody was into it, as the title flashed over a frozen image of Sam in mid flight: Hot Fun. A Rodeo Snow Production.

"What's a Rodeo Snow?" Lily asked and everyone said Shhh! as Sam's image dropped to the ground. Brady entered the screen and the music moved to "Woman with the Tattooed Hands," by Atmosphere, as he ground a rail. There was a section of me doing a flawless tweaked flat spin as Andy had promised. Of course, I edited out the ones where I wiped out.

Using my editorial privilege, I decided not to put myself in the bail section. I kept thinking Corinne might see this and for some reason it really annoyed me to think of her and Andy curled up together on some couch watching my screw ups.

Everybody clapped at the end. Dad whistled when these images, of Andy on his board and me on my skates, flew through the air, collided, then seemed to go through each other and reappear on opposite sides.

"Wait," Andy said. "We've got something else." The camera zoomed in on a blender. You couldn't tell at first but when it got close up, you could see that there was a big coil of a turd lodged in the blades.

"Gross," Lilly piped up. Leave it to Lily to zero in on what was wrong with this picture.

"Disgusting!" said Sam.

"Eeww!" said Brady.

Dad shook his head.

Only Mom didn't have a clue. "What is this?" she asked. "A cooking class? A science project?"

"It's poop in a blender," Andy announced, obviously pleased with himself. All of the sudden, it started whirring around to Elvis singing "All Shook Up."

"That is evil," said Sam.

"Thanks," said Andy. Mom was speechless as the screen spinned with shit.

"Liquify," Andy explained with a straight face. That did it. I exploded with laughter. Andy lost it too. We practically fell on the floor laughing, as Lily covered her eyes and moaned.

"Where did you get that blender?" Mom demanded.

"Where did you get that turd?" Brady blurted out, then covered his mouth as my mom gave him her kindergarten teacher I have the power to determine the rest of your life and I feel like using it look.

"Don't worry, Mom," I tried to reassure her. "It's not ours." I meant the blender. I wasn't about to divulge the turd sources.

"Where did you get that blender?"

"Uh, it's mine." Andy hung his head. I saw my dad shaking with silent laughter. The thing was that every kid in the room, except for me and Lily, had my mom as their kindergarten teacher. And Lily and I had her as our kindergarten teacher for life. We all regressed to age five, and everyone in the room was in deep crap even the ones who didn't do it. The poop in a blender was still on the screen, looking so disgusting you could almost smell it.

"Yours, as in you bought it?"

"Well, not exactly." Andy hung his head even lower, trying not to laugh.

"Yours, as in you got it from your mother's cupboard?"

"I rinsed it when we were done." Andy beamed at her like a dumb dog who just dropped a dead animal at his owner's feet.

"Rinsed it?" Mom raised her voice. "In our kitchen sink?"

"I think I'm going to throw up," Lily announced.

Andy ignored her, "Naah, in the bathroom sink. After I, you know, dumped the, you know, in the toilet."

"And where is this blender?" Mom asked.

"I put it right back in the cupboard where I found it," Andy said proudly. This made me wonder if he only paid attention to half the lessons in kindergarten.

Everybody groaned.

"I'm calling your mother right now." Mom turned toward the kitchen. "I'm thinking of sending her a sympathy card."

"That's cold, Mrs. Snow," Sam called out.

Everyone nodded in agreement. Except Lily, the butt kisser, who said, "I'm going to make her one." She followed my mom into the kitchen.

"Why do you guys enjoy torturing your mothers?" Dad asked.

"It's entertaining," Andy said.

"We wouldn't do it if they didn't get so worked up," I added.

"Mrs. Snow is so funny when she gets mad," Brady agreed. "Remember how we'd spy on the girls in the bathroom just to get them to scream? She told me once if I did that one more time, she'd make me use the girls' bathroom just so they'd get used to me."

Everyone laughed, except for me, because I, of course, was across the hall with Mrs. Bagley, who should have retired ten years earlier. All I could remember about kindergarten was my legs falling asleep when we had to sit tailor style on the rug for hours.

Mom returned, after a few minutes, phone in hand, saying, "I'll take the two of them out to buy a new blender. They can split the cost."

I sighed, knowing that my mom would make us buy an expensive gourmet one.

She got off the phone. "Okay, who wants cake?"

Lily walked in, carefully balancing a chocolate frosted layer cake in her arms.

"Cake!" My friends crowded around Lily like a pigs at a trough.

"Move it or I'll drop it!" Lily threatened. They backed off immediately. That girl definitely had the bossy teacher gene.

"Wait," Lily ordered, "I'll get the candles." She set the cake on the dining room table and walked back to the kitchen.

"Is it someone's birthday?" Sam asked.

"Not really," I muttered.

"Actually it was my birthday on Tuesday and Lily wanted to make a cake for today," Mom said, blushing. Even she got that this was weird.

"You brought presents, didn't you?" Dad deadpanned.

"Hey, nobody said this was a birthday party," said Sam, taking him seriously.

"Kathy likes money if you have any on you," Dad continued, obviously enjoying himself.

"Ray! Stop it!" Mom ordered.

"It's a joke," I said as Sam stared at them.

Lily came back and started poking about a million candles all over the cake so it looked like a pastel-needled porcupine.

"Just how old are you, Mrs. S.?" Brady asked.

"I don't think you've had enough math yet to comprehend her age," Dad said.

"You keep up with your little jokes, and there'll be no cake for you," Mom threatened.

Dad pretended to look worried and lit the candles, even the ones that stuck out on the sides. "I think you better blow them out before we sing or this cake's gonna be one big ball of wax," he told her.

"Wait!" Lily insisted, closing the shades for a better candle-lit atmosphere. Mom huffed and puffed and practically blew the cake down.

Everybody sang the Birthday Bongo which, of course, all my friends remembered from kindergarten. Even Sam, who was way too cool for such things, was belting it out, which made me realize he must have been making fun of her. I half-heartedly sang along. Then I realized they were making fun of her because it was the only way they could save face and get to sing this song, which they seemed to really want to do. I wondered if Mom understood.

She did seem embarrassed by all the attention. I gave her credit for that. Even though she seemed happily embarrassed. "Do you want to eat cake, or not," she griped, as we held the final note as long and off key as possible. We wanted to eat the cake.

"I loved kindergarten," Brady rhapsodized, as he took a big bite of cake, which left him with a frosting mustache.

Lily and I looked at each other. The L girl and I had this in common: everybody loved kindergarten except us because we spent the year in the dud classroom.

As everybody was leaving, Sam turned to Mom and said, "Mrs. Snow, what's with the billboard in your front yard?"

Mom beamed. "You mean our lawn sign?"

"Billboard." Dad agreed with Sam. I'd heard him tell Mom it was so big it obstructed traffic and could cause an accident.

"I've got smaller ones in the garage if your parents want one," Mom offered.

"Sure," Sam said smoothly like he really wanted one.

I was mortified because my mom should have known Sam's parents wouldn't be caught dead with a political sign in their yard. But Mom could be really stupid. She went to get one. "Anyone else?"

"We only support communists in our family," Brady said.

I decided not to mention that, *by the way Mom, not everyone cares about this stuff. And I would appreciate it if you didn't try to force your politics on my friends who are just going to trash your signs anyway.* I knew enough to avoid her usual mind-numbing lecture on the importance of the democratic process and the responsibility we all had to be good citizens.

Anyway, I avoided arguing with Mom by avoiding her until I was ready to take off that night. I was meeting my friends at the White Sand Beach. She started with her usual question that was really a lecture about how there wasn't going to be alcohol or drugs there, right?

And I said right, because there wasn't, at least not with my group of friends. Then I started out the door and she sprung it on me: "Gene," she said, "something's been bothering me about your video."

I sighed and wondered why she had to take the poop in a blender bit so seriously. "Mom, it was just a joke. A visual joke."

"Oh, not the blender," she said, but her forehead was all wrinkled up in worry, which had me worried. "This flyer was in our mailbox today." She waved a paper in front of me that said in big, scribbly pissed-off letters, "STOP DESTRUCTION OF CHURCH PROPERTY. NO SKATING ON THE CONVENT STAIRS. THIS MEANS YOUR KID."

"Wow, that's nasty," I said.

"A lot of your video was filmed on the Stairs, " Mom pointed out. "Are you bothering the nuns?"

"Not unless they can't handle being around people who are having fun."

"I don't want to hear that you're being disrespectful to anyone, Gene."

"Yes, ma'am," I said, in an overly respectful way.

"Gene," Mom warned, as I backed out the door.

"Gotta go, Mom. Tomorrow's Labor Day. Then school. Remember?" I made my escape into the steamy end of the summer night where the White Sand Beach of the Mississippi was waiting.

CHAPTER FOUR
BUM BUSTERS

I skated to River Road, then sat on a bench by the railroad bridge changing into my shoes and hooking my skates to my backpack. I hoped Andy or somebody would come along soon because it was getting darker. I could've headed down the path into the woods at the river's edge, but I'd never gone there by myself. Just the thought of it gave me the creeps. Every once in a while, we'd walked past bums, homeless guys down there.

"Hey!" Someone plopped down beside me, making me jump up about a mile. "I am so glad to see you," Corinne said.

"Oh, hi," I said, trying to act nonchalant and not like I was totally relieved to see her.

"You know the way?" She stood up and turned toward the woods.

"Sure," I said. "Just waiting for Andy."

"He's probably down there already." Corinne once again assumed she was the expert when she knew nothing.

"We usually wait up here until everybody comes," I said.

"You guys sure are a bunch of chickenshits." She shook her head so her hair fell forward into her face.

It annoyed me she just left a strand of it rippling down her cheek so it caught the light of the street lamp. I had to fight an impulse to reach toward her and brush it back with my fingers or treat her like that brat Lily and yank it.

Instead I shrugged. "We can go down, but I bet they'll stay up here waiting for us."

"Right."

The things I do to pretend I'm not the nerd I really I am, I thought, as I turned toward the dirt path and led the way into the darkness.

"Hey," Corinne complained. "You got a flashlight?"

"No." I stopped and looked back at her. I was not prepared and proud of it. "Flashlights are for chickenshits."

She snorted and put her hands on her hips. I turned back to the path, smiling to myself. I heard her grumbling after I accidentally on purpose let a branch whip past me and catch her.

"Nice!" Corinne said when we scrambled down the last jog in the path and reached the river.

I knew what she meant, but nice wasn't the word I would've used. I would've said magic. The metal skeleton of the railroad bridge hovered beyond us. The river, dark and muddy, wound past. The moon came out from behind a bank of clouds so the gritty sand on the beach gave off this blue light like houses I skated past late at night, lit only by the glow of a TV screen. It felt dangerous there and I kind of liked it.

Corinne lit a cigarette and held the pack out to me.

"No thanks," I said, but, for a second, I wished I did smoke. It fit with the atmosphere. The red end of Corinne's cigarette stood out like a dot of color in a black-and-white movie. We sat on opposite ends of a log and silently watched the river, breathing in its end-of-summer stink mingled with cigarette smoke. It smelled like someone had set fire to a compost pile and it was quietly smoldering. Not that it smelled bad. It actually smelled good in a sad way. It smelled like summer was rotting and giving way to fall, school, new things.

I wanted that moment to last forever but just as I thought that, the rest of my friends clomped down the path grouching in loud voices. I glanced at Corinne to see if she was as disgusted as I was that the spell had been broken. She, of course, jumped up and put her arms around Andy.

"You guys missed running into that bum—what a loser," Sam said.

"Yeah. We should find his camp and firebomb it," Brady said. They arranged firewood they'd brought from Brady's house, adding twigs and garbage from the woods for kindling.

"Take that bum man," Sam announced, as he threw a lit match on the fire. The crumpled up newspaper and candy bar wrappers burst into flame, and my friends laughed in this harsh way that sounded like crows cawing.

"Just what did this guy do?" Corinne asked.

"He went psycho when he saw us heading down the path," Brady said.

"He was insane," Andy said. "It was like he had rabies. He was almost foaming at the mouth."

"He just kept saying, 'Get out, get out. This is private property,' and shaking a stick at us. So we headed down fast," Sam added. "Good thing he didn't sneak up on you."

"What did he do when you came down anyway?" I asked, nervously looking back at the woods, half expecting the guy to appear there.

"I whipped out my cell phone and told him I had the police programmed on speed dial," said Andy.

"He freaked and took off at that," Sam said.

"My hero." Corinne squeezed closer to Andy.

"Hey, I would have taken care of things if he'd shown up here," I insisted.

"You would've bailed," Corinne laughed.

"Gene would've had his mother invite the guy over for dinner." Sam got into it.

"Shut up." Everybody cracked up and hooted. "Just because she'd let a loser like you in our house."

"He really was crazy," Andy said seriously. "I wish I could call the police but then we'd get busted too."

"That's why we need to rely on a little vigilante justice," Brady said. "I've got some fireworks." Like this was something new—Brady was a pyromaniac who always stuffed his pack with the latest explosives he'd bought in Wisconsin. "We could find his camp and, you know, not hurt him or anything, just scare him."

"What if he's like got a gun or something?" I asked.

"He's just crazy," Andy assured me. "Just a harmless crazy guy."

I didn't feel so good about that but I told myself I'd probably feel different if I'd been verbally assaulted by this guy. Plus everybody was making me out to be a mama's boy.

"We can't let some psycho tell us we can't be here," Corinne insisted. "We have just as much right to be here as he does. Even more. We pay taxes."

Everyone hooted in approval, but I couldn't let that pass. "Taxes?" I said, "Since when do fifteen-year-olds pay taxes? Just how much do you pay in taxes, Corinne?"

"My parents pay taxes." Corinne wasn't backing down. "Every dollar they pay in taxes is a dollar out of my pocket."

My friends were impressed by that. I could see them doing the mental arithmetic, trying to figure out how much money the government was bilking them out of.

"Let's take care of business." Brady pulled a giant Roman candle out of his pack. Sam went for some river water to put out the fire. Corinne hugged Andy excited at the thought of terrorizing some old homeless guy, and Andy who knew a good deal when he saw it, hugged her back.

So, you're hanging out with your best friends in the whole world and this girl who for some reason has gotten into your brain like an earwig in an old *Star Trek* movie. All you want to do is enjoy the last night of summer. Enjoy it with your friends who may stop being your friends if you don't help them firebomb some poor, hopefully defenseless, bum's camp. What do you do?

A. Prove to them you're no chickenshit and join the gang to ambush this guy.

B. Prove to yourself you're no chickenshit by making a speech refusing to go that's so convincing they see the error of their ways.

C. Do what your parents have always told you is right and responsible: go report what's going on to a "caring" adult.

D. Run away like the chickenshit that deep down you know you really are.

Well, what I figured was no fifteen-year-old, no matter how morally superior, parentally indoctrinated or just plain chicken was anything without his friends. I went along with them, hoping if I sighed, it would mean I was reluctant and therefore a little less guilty, hoping that the moon would stay behind the clouds and we wouldn't find the guy.

"Shh," Sam hissed. "If you don't stop breathing so loud, Gene, we're not gonna surprise him."

"Sorry," I said, even though I wasn't sorry at all.

"Shhhh!" Everybody turned back at me, and Sam poked me hard in the ribs with his elbow. I bit my tongue and didn't even say ow. I took a deep breath as quietly as I could. The air didn't smell bittersweet and magical anymore. It just smelled rotten.

Suddenly, everybody got real quiet and stopped. We were up on a little hill and had a good view of the guy. He had long straggly hair and a ratty beard and was muttering to himself crouching by an almost dead fire.

"Poor dude," Andy said. "He is so out of his mind."

Sam passed Corinne's lighter to Brady who lit the Roman candle and aimed the tube so that it started shooting exploding fireballs at the guy. We stood mesmerized as he jumped up and howled. It was like watching your own private horror movie. It was like the sound of an animal that didn't usually make a sound. Like a rabbit screaming. It got even more freaky when we realized that he saw us.

Now I was in total chickenshit mode. I ran out of the woods as fast as I could to what I hoped was still the safety of my neighborhood, vowing never to breathe a word about this to anyone. My friends ran in front of me laughing like this was the funniest thing they'd ever seen.

"That was tight!" Sam whooped.

"Did you see the look on his face?" Brady asked when we reached River Road. "He looked like he must've crapped his pants."

"He was so scared. He won't bother us anymore," said Sam.

"He'll probably leave the state," bragged Corinne. "Hey, we could start a business. Bum Eradication."

"Bum Busters!" Andy joined in, and they all started laughing again. Everybody except me. I half ran behind them, trying to figure out what the bum's face, all contorted and freaked out, lit by the exploding fire reminded me of. Then it came to me and I stood still as I remembered: my mom's face that afternoon, glowing over the forest of birthday candles, open-mouthed and vulnerable, like a little kid at our mercy for her happiness.

CHAPTER FIVE

THE SCENE OF THE CRIME

Labor Day was the least fun holiday I knew. I stayed in my room most of the day, feeling the irony of having absolutely nothing to do with the last free time I'd have for forever.

"Gene," Mom yelled up to me. "Andy's at the front door."

"Tell him I'm cleaning my room and can't come out," I yelled back, knowing there was no way she'd let anyone interrupt that. Then I wadded up a candy bar wrapper, aimed for the waste basket and missed. I snuck a peek out the window and watched Andy trudge away, carrying his skateboard. He looked bored to the core.

"Sorry, dude," I muttered, "but I'm in no mood to entertain you."

I still felt bad about the night before. I scanned the entire paper that morning to make sure there wasn't an article about a fire by the river or a homeless man getting burned. Maybe no news was good news. Or maybe his camp was destroyed and nobody really cared enough to mention it. I tossed a dirty sock toward the empty laundry basket, then decided I'd done enough cleaning for the day.

I headed downstairs and put on my skates. Maybe if I made sure that bum was okay, I could stop feeling guilty and get in some good skating.

"Gene?" Mom said from the kitchen. "I thought you were cleaning your room."

"Done." I skated toward the door.

"Wonderful." I heard her voice behind me. I headed out, double checking to make sure Andy was long gone.

I cruised to the river and realized—critical detail—I forgot my shoes. I took off my skates and stowed them under a bush and headed down in my socks. This was pretty miserable since my feet kept landing on rocks and exposed roots. As I got close to the camp, all of a sudden, I realized that I didn't have the slightest idea what I was going to find or what I was going to do.

You come across a burnt, charred, barely recognizable as human, body in the woods, contorted in agony beside a cold camp fire and call 911 (after you throw up). What do you tell them?

A. You just happened to find a dead body as you were going for a stroll in the woods in your socks.
B. You're an accomplice to murder and, by the way, here's the names of your friends who lit and aimed the murder weapon.
C. They need to check the woods by the railroad bridge. Then hang up.

The options, as usual, sucked. I stood there, for a minute, then made myself go on until I reached the clearing. It was weirdly empty. The bum's shopping cart was gone. The ground was all burnt but at least nothing was still burning. I relaxed and told myself this was good. If the bum was hurt or dead, the police would've roped off the area with plastic caution ribbons. He must've been in good enough shape to cover his tracks and ditch the place. I stepped into the center of the black shadow of the fire pit and tried to figure out how much of it was campfire, how much firework damage. It didn't look so bad in daylight. In fact, it looked like someone just had a really big campfire.

Just then the hairs stood up on the back of my neck. Someone was watching me. I turned around but there was no one there. Then I heard a rustling. And there he was: the bum, coming toward me from the bushes, dressed in a filthy camouflage suit, shaking a tree branch in front of him like it was a skeleton arm.

"You're one of them," he accused, his twitchy rabbity eyes glinting.

"I don't know what you're talking about." I tried to back away from him but found myself frozen with fear like I was in a bad dream. I kept hearing his scream from the other night. Like the sound you hear in your head when you're so scared you open your mouth and nothing comes out.

"Why are you torturing me?" He moved closer.

"I don't know what you're talking about," I insisted. But he kept moving toward me. "I'll get you some money," I blurted out. "How much do you need?"

"Money?" He laughed, his mouth making a black hole in his scraggly beard. He was so close I could smell his sour breath. "Do you think your money can stop them from torturing me?" He poked me with his stick. Then dropped it and grabbed my shoulders. "Why can't you leave me alone?" he asked. He smelled like every bad smell I'd ever smelled combined. Sort of like a human garbage can. And he looked like something out of *Night of the Living Dead* which made me hold my breath and close my eyes.

"Leave me alone," he yelled and started shaking me. I pushed him away, which broke the spell he had over me. I ran back to the place where I hid my skates. But he was too fast and caught up with me. He grabbed my skates. I tried to grab them back but he was so strong he pulled me toward him.

"Give me my skates." I tugged at him, as he laughed at me, his breath so bad it made me gag.

He lifted up my skates like a weapon and just missed my head. At that point I gave up and ran. I ran until I ran into Andy.

"There you are." He grinned. "Hey, what's the matter?"

"It's that bum," I explained. "He took my skates." And I told him what had happened.

"He probably grabbed them just to scare you," Andy said. "I bet he left them there."

"Andy," I said, hoping this wouldn't be as big of a deal to him as it seemed to me. "Could you go check by the bushes? You could do it fast on your skateboard."

"No problem," he said and took off, leaving me to wait on a street corner in my socks, hoping no one would notice me.

It took forever for him to get back which, of course, gave me time to imagine all sorts of things: Andy attacked by the rabid bum who was frothing at the mouth. Andy ambushed by the police who were waiting for some juvenile delinquent to return to the scene of the crime. All I could think about were the dumb choices I had made and how they seemed to be rolled up in a ball that was growing bigger and faster and heading straight toward me.

"Are you okay?" I looked up from my seat on some stranger's lawn to see a policeman sticking his head out the window of his cop car.

I almost said no and blurted out how I could of killed this old homeless guy or burned his face off but instead I let him steal my incredibly expensive, almost new Shima 3 skates, which I would never be able to replace and my parents would kill me when they found out, and I just sent my best friend to his doom which may have been okay since I tended to blame him for the whole thing anyway. But instead I heard myself saying, "Yeah . . . I mean, yes sir, just waiting for someone." I glanced down at my socks which seemed to be shouting "something's wrong with this picture, officer, arrest him."

But the policeman just smiled and shook his head. "Girlfriend running late? Hope she didn't stand you up, son."

Girlfriend? This was how somebody looked when they had a girlfriend? Confused, miserable, guilty and missing critical clothing items? I started to say something, but he rolled up his window and moved on.

"No luck, Gene." Andy skated up from the other direction empty-handed. "There's no sign of your skates, of the bum, of anything. Maybe it's all a bad dream and like none of it ever happened."

"Right. You want to tell that to my parents? You want to tell them I lost my skates when I was out sleepwalking?"

Andy shrugged. "Well at least that crazy guy's okay. I was kind of feeling bad about what we did to him."

"Yeah," I agreed, thinking that at least the two things I was worried about: hurting that old bum and finding out that Andy wasn't who I thought he was, turned out all right. I couldn't believe I had to lose my skates to find this out though. "Are you sure you looked in the right place?" I asked.

"Well, yeah. I checked the bushes. I even went down the path."

I started pacing. Andy shook his head. "Calm down."

Okay, so I was starting to freak out. I was walking back and forth in my socks, waving my arms around. "How can I calm down? Do you know how much those skates cost? And they're customized. What do you think—that I can find a pair just like them in the used bin at *Play It Again Sports?*"

"Gene, stop spazzing. The police are driving by. You look like that crazy bum with your arms flapping."

"I'll spaz if I want to." I stretched my arms to the sky for emphasis. "Like you would be all calm if some old bum just stole your $300 pair of skates."

"Everything all right, boys?" The same cop as before hung his head out his car window.

"He's just gesticulating officer," Andy explained. Leave it to Andy to think one of his eighth-grade vocabulary words will convince an authority figure we're just a couple of harmless nerds. "It helps him get out his frustration."

The policeman wrinkled his brow, then nodded. "Guess that girl never showed up. Don't get too worked up about her, son. She's not worth it."

"I guess you're right, sir." I shoved my hands in my pockets and tried to look like I was taking his advice.

He drove away and I turned to Andy. "'He's just gesticulating, officer?' You made it sound I was doing something obscene. Are you trying to get us thrown in jail?"

"What girl?" Andy ignored me. "You're waiting for a girl?"

The next morning, in first-hour American Government, I found I was waiting for a girl, hoping against my better judgment Corinne would show up. I didn't realize this until she walked in and collapsed at the desk next to Andy's. Like the day was already too much for her even though it had just started.

CHAPTER SIX

BAREFOOT IN A
BAD SITUATION

I watched Corinne. I couldn't help watching Corinne, in her tight black T-shirt, eyes droopy with sleep and a ton of eye makeup, perk up when this long-haired guy walked in, then jumped halfway across the room, landing seated on the teacher's desk. The class suddenly became quiet as he joked, "don't try this at home." Then he leapt up and wrote on the board, "AP AMERICAN GOVERNMENT, MR. MAC, E PLURIBUS UNUM."

"I'm Mr. McKenzie. But I go by Mr. Mac," he announced. "This is first-hour Advanced Placement American Government. Anyone who's in the wrong place is welcome to leave." No one moved. Even Brady, who had hyperactively drummed his pencil on every desk since first grade, sat frozen.

"If, after reading the syllabus, you think you should be in a remedial class," he continued, now moving from row to row, flinging out papers like frisbees, "realize that you have a lot of company. Fifty-eight percent of adults when surveyed don't have a clue as to who their senators and representatives are but eighty-nine percent can name who won on *American Idol*." He paused to let that disgusting tidbit of trivia sink in.

"Anyone here able to provide the names of your representatives?" He stood in front of his desk, his eyes boring into us. I couldn't look at him. Instead I found myself staring at his tie, which was as conservative as his black frizzed-out hair was wild and crazy.

45

The class sat in silence. Some kid behind me yawned really loud and a couple of kids laughed. Mr. Mac went over to the board and erased the AP in front of American Government and wrote after it: For Dummies, in big letters. This was totally unfair. After all, I knew the answers. Like I could've lived with my family and not have that stuff ooze into me by osmosis. But it was 8:30 in the morning and my brain didn't start functioning until noon. Besides, I wasn't giving Derek Martin, the giant dickhead sitting across from me the satisfaction of saying I learned this stuff from my kindergarten teacher mommy. Which he would've done in a loud voice, I could guarantee.

"Excuse me." This girl with this fake sounding European accent, raised her hand.

"Yes, Ms . . . ?" Mr. Mac paused for her name.

She rattled off something totally unpronounceable, sounding like she was clearing her throat. "Please call me Lark," she said. "Americans have such a difficult time pronouncing my name." She put us all down with a pink lipsticked smile, then rattled off the names of our senators, state and federal, and the federal representative for our district. "I am not certain of these." She shrugged like she was modest, which obviously she wasn't.

"Frenchie," Derek Martin whispered, like he was both flirting with and insulting her.

"I have only been in your country one month from Belgium." She glared at Derek. "I speak Dutch."

"Well." Mr. Mac was obviously impressed. "How about the rest of you? Have you all been in our country only one month?"

That did it. I raised my hand.

"Mr . . ." Mr. Mac called on me.

"Snow," I said. "She," I nodded at Lark, who flashed me her neon pink smile, "forgot to mention our state representative." I gave his name and then explained that the state and

46

federal representatives and state senators were different depending on what district you lived in.

Some girl genius, who was waiting for it to be acceptable to open her mouth, added that the state senator, who Lark named, wouldn't be up for re-election because she was running for lieutenant governor.

"Yes!" Mr. Mac pounded his fist on his desk, causing me to jump about a foot in the air. "Re-election! People, we have a great opportunity this fall to study our electoral process in action. But that means we have to put the pedal to the metal and learn the basics about how our political system works first. If you look at the syllabus, you'll see I'm expecting you to read chapters one through four in the textbook by tomorrow. There will also be a quiz on your state and federal legislators. But before you think you can get off easy and regurgitate Ms. Lark and Mr. Snow's list, remember you may have different state legislators, depending on your address."

I grinned at Andy because I, of course, got off easier than the rest of the class. "Oh, and Mr. Snow," he added, "I'm bumping you up to AP status. You can report for us on who's running for what statewide offices in this election. Including third parties."

I sighed. Corinne whispered, "That's what you get—suckup."

"Did you have a question Ms . . . ?"

"Camden," she said, totally smoothly, like she'd been waiting for him to call on her. "Yeah, I was wondering what the words meant. You know, those Greek ones you wrote on the board."

"Latin," he said. "Thank you, Ms. Camden. I'm glad someone's paying attention."

I didn't get it. Here I saved this class from looking like the losers they were, and I got extra homework, while Corinne had everybody fooled and fawning all over her.

Derek Martin, Mr. I am God's Gift to the Universe, raised his hand. "It means kind of like United We Stand."

Mr. Mac nodded, "United We Stand is close. The literal translation is 'Out of Many, One,' as in a national government formed by uniting many states. Does anyone remember seeing this slogan before the ubiquitous 911 bumper stickers and muscle shirts?"

You got me. I glanced over at Andy, who I was sure knew the answer to everything we'd discussed so far, but was keeping his mouth shut in this kind of perverse reverse non show off show for Corinne.

"E Pluribus Unum is on money," Derek said. He reached in his pocket and pulled out a quarter which everyone squinted at like they could really read the miniscule print.

"Excellent, Mr. . . ."

"Derek." He cocked his head at what he thought was an attractive angle and looked at the girls behind him before he finished. But Mr. Mac was on fast forward and interrupted him.

"Well, Mr. Derek," he said, as he paced back and forth in front of the class. I snorted and some kids laughed.

"Martin," Derek added.

Mr. Mac shook his head and sighed. "Mr. Derek Martin, you have been promoted to AP status with Mr. Snow and can do the same assignment. We'll discuss the origin and significance of the phrase E Pluribus Unum tomorrow. Oh, and by the way, please note that I don't grade on a curve. There's a certain level of knowledge and critical thinking I expect in this class and I'm not going to lower my standards to the lowest common denominator. Those of you who follow reality TV can think of this class as *Survivor* revisited." We all groaned and trudged out the door, weighted down by the monster books he passed out and the miserable year outlined on his syllabus.

As we headed down the crowded hall to our next classes, Corinne griped, "It isn't fair. You guys have lived here your entire lives, so of course you know about all these political figures." She said it like they were action figures. Like we had watched more *Pokemon* than she had so we were able to memorize the characters.

"How am I supposed to find this stuff out by tomorrow?" she said, ignoring the fact that even the girl from another country knew more than she did.

We tried to cut across the commons but came to a stop because it was so crowded. Sometimes high school seemed like preparation for going to work in a traffic jam. We elbowed our way forward. "You could ask him if you could list your Chicago ones since you've lived there your entire life," I suggested, exposing her excuse for the lame thing it was.

"Right," she said, not admitting she didn't have a clue about the names of any politician. I got this feeling she might flunk that reality test they give people in the hospital when they ask who's the president of the United States.

"I'll go ask him for you." I started turning back as we climbed the stairs but got pushed forward. We were just like the endless line of bugs in that movie *Antz*.

"You asshole. You'd better not say anything to him!" She slugged me in the arm as we reached the hallway.

"Ouch! You try to help a poor pathetic girl and what does she do but beat you up."

Andy who was walking with us, more like Corinne's extra body part than the person I knew, started laughing.

"Hey, you're supposed to be on my side." Corinne slugged him too and a goofy lovesick grin spread across his face.

"I don't know what you're getting so worked up about." He finally let himself sound smart. "It goes by address, remember? Since we live right by Gene, we have the same reps as he does."

"Oh, yeah." Corinne nodded as we walked into our sociology class. She sat down, ripped a page out of her notebook and started writing. "Okay, tell me who they are again, Mr. Snow."

"Gee." I wrinkled my forehead, as the last bell rang. "I can't seem to remember."

"I'm gonna kill you," she mouthed as the class started.

No, I thought. *Andy will give you the names, and you'll tell him he's your big hunky hero and you'll spend the evening wrapped around each other on your couch in front of the TV. And you'll pretend to read the American Government assignment while Andy really reads it and summarizes it for you.*

I ended up walking home with Sam and Brady as the buses rumbled past us. They'd cut our bus service, and the quickest way home was on a busy street, through an industrial wasteland. We had to walk single file on the shoulder of Hiawatha Avenue, hoping that nobody would run us over.

"You're the oldest, Gene. You've got to get your license and buy a car," Sam said. "Take your test on your birthday and get your parents to buy you a car as a present."

"Right." I rolled my eyes.

In home room that morning, the teacher announced that there were only thirteen lockers for thirty-nine kids. I got stuck sharing with that hyper-perfect Belgian girl. Then they tripled up some kids and had us share with Brady. Now I got to look forward to a year of my stuff smelling like a cross between B.O. and perfume. And I knew Miss Perfectly Organized and Mr. Cloud of Filth Around Him wouldn't get along at all and guess who would be stuck in the middle.

Plus, I had homework in almost every class and Algebra II promised to be the hardest math class I'd ever had. And I had to lug all this stuff home. Maybe they should've just assigned homework by weight instead of pages.

Even though I had a load of homework and my mom would've accused me of getting off to a lousy start, I had to blow it off for as long as possible and skate, or I was afraid I might shrivel up and die. I read that Chris Edwards practiced six hours a day. I bet he never had to do homework.

I squeezed on my old skates, then decided I'd better take off my socks or they'd never fit. They weren't bad barefoot. I skated to the Stairs, which were deserted, and jumped down the concrete slope into a cess slide. I braked sideways on both skates like a hockey stop. Screeching to a stop again and again, trying to get the bad day I had out of my system.

"I was wondering when you'd show up again," a voice said behind me. I felt this sick shiver go through me. I'd been watching the wood doors the whole time. She must have come from the side.

"Sorry." I started to skate off.

"Wait!" the old lady ordered. I felt myself stop and turn around like I was under her creepy spell. "What's your name?" she asked.

"Gene," I muttered. "Gene Snow." Why did I tell her the truth? I should have said my name was Derek Martin. Then if she stuck pins in a voodoo doll, good old Derek would've gotten it.

"Gene. As in Eugene?" She fidgeted and dug in her pocket.

"Yes, ma'am."

"Sister." She pulled out a cigarette and lit it. "Sister Jude."

"Yes, Sister." I wondered if nuns were allowed to smoke. But this was definitely one nun who didn't care about the rules. Unless they were her rules.

"I want to offer you a job, Eugene."

51

"Uh, no thanks," I said, hardly believing I was turning down a job, a real job I didn't even have to apply for.

"Honey." She shook her head. I liked it better when she called me Eugene. "Honey, I wish you'd stop acting like I'm asking you to help me sacrifice small children. It's a good job." She put out her cigarette and pocketed the butt which I was sure she'd smoke later. "Come in my office and I'll show you."

All of the sudden it occurred to me that the *Simpsons* would be on soon, that I had to do my homework, that I was wearing skates with no socks, and I wasn't sure if it was okay for someone like me to go into a convent. I tried to think back to who was allowed in to where Julie Andrews lived in *The Sound of Music*, but I hadn't seen that movie in a long time.

"Just take off your skates," Sister Jude said, as I hesitated at the big wooden door.

"But I'm barefoot."

"And what do you think Jesus wore on his feet?" she demanded.

"Sandals?"

She laughed, this big explosive hah that echoed into the dark space beyond the door. "Sandals! What kind of yuppie Protestant are you?"

"Um, I'm Unitarian."

"Unitarian!" She laughed again. "I suppose you think Jesus wore Birkenstocks."

I looked over at her feet while I pulled off my skates. She was barefoot just like the other day.

I followed her through this gloomy little chapel lit by candles in red glasses. Then down this claustrophobic staircase to her office in the basement.

There were mountains of paper on the desk, on the floor. The ceiling was all spidery with cobwebs. The big black phone on the desk actually had a dial on it. And I felt eyes looking at me from every direction. They stared from paintings, posters, statues, knickknacks. I had to get out of there. Why did I keep finding myself barefoot in bad situations?

Sister Jude dug through a pile of papers that looked like the Leaning Tower of Pisa. "Angels and martyrs," she said as she noticed me getting freaked out. "I collect them . . . or maybe they collect me. My only vice." She shrugged.

I laughed nervously. This creepy statue with blank eyes looked at me like I was the one with the vices.

Sister Jude frowned. "I suppose you think smoking is a vice."

Duh, I thought, but I didn't dare say a thing.

"It's a bad habit I returned to when I started working with the poor. When poor people can afford nicotine patches and don't need to resort to crisis behavior, I'll quit."

So when hell freezes over. The eyes continued to stare at me.

"There it is." She pulled handed me a piece of paper.

"Nice," I said, glad I could honestly compliment her on this really professional drawing.

"It's a fence," she explained.

"Yeah. It's a good drawing." It kind of reminded me of what my dad drew when he was planning to build something.

"To go around the steps into the convent," she added. "To keep out the roller skaters." I didn't say anything. I felt like I had entered *The Twilight Zone*.

"Of course, I wouldn't be able to pay you in cash," she said, confirming I was in what must have been some kind of bizarre alternate universe. She looked at me with her yellowish-green owl eyes. The angels and the tortured saints looked at me, as if they expected me to be hypnotized into submission.

A spooky old nun asks you to help her build a fence for free, a fence to keep you and your friends out of the only decent skating place in the neighborhood. What do you do?

A. Say "Why certainly, Sister, I'd love to join your group of zombified angels and help keep the riffraff out of your creepy paradise."
B. Explain "I'm sorry, Sister, but did I mention to you that I have an incurable disease that makes it impossible for me to hold anything as heavy as a hammer? But since I'm in crisis, could I bum a cigarette?"
C. Yell "NO WAY" and run. Get the hell out of there.

I was just about to opt for C when she did something that changed everything. She reached to the back of a cluttered shelf and pulled out my Shimas. She plunked them down on her desk and said, "I can't afford to pay cash, but I thought we might barter." She smiled like she thought she was being nice or something.

I considered grabbing the skates and running anyway, yelling, "They're mine, you psycho!" But just then I heard a noise. I turned to find him standing at the door: the bum from the river, tensed and ready to spring like a wild animal.

"Eugene," she said, "This is Billy, the draftsman you'll be working with." She introduced him like he was some famous architect or something. I cringed, waiting for him to start yelling at me. But he was quiet, looking down at my skates, the ones he took and I had to earn back. Sister Jude walked between us and put an arm around each of our shoulders. "This would be a good learning experience for you, Eugene. Billy could really teach you something."

CHAPTER SEVEN
LOST CAUSES

"You're not gonna do it, are you?" Brady asked.

"You can't do it," Corinne insisted.

I was afraid of this. Afraid my friends would see the fence building from their side of the fence. The outside.

"Any other brilliant ideas how I can get my skates back?" I asked, hiking my pack, which felt like it was stuffed with bricks instead of books, up on my shoulder. We were walking home from school and the cars on Hiawatha Avenue whizzed past us just to point out our slow motion drudgery.

"Steal them," Brady suggested.

"Right." I kicked some gravel in disgust.

"It's better than your building this stupid fence to wall us out of the only decent skate place within walking distance," Corinne said. All she was carrying was a little purse that swung from her shoulder and bumped her hip in rhythm as she walked. I found myself craning my neck as we walked in single file just to watch it. Swing, bump, swing. It was hypnotizing. I walked a little faster, then slowed down once we got to a regular sidewalk, just so I could walk directly behind her.

"Like we can go there anymore anyway," I argued. "Sister Jude watches the Stairs twenty-four hours a day with her evil eye."

"Sister Jude." Andy readjusted his pack, which was so crammed with stuff, he looked like a bum hauling everything he owned on his back. I wondered if he was doing something as pathetic as carrying Corinne's books for her. Doubtful. Corinne probably thought she was above studying.

"Jude is the patron saint of hopeless causes," Andy informed us. He was always spouting these obscure, random facts. He started nah, nahing, singing the refrain from that Beatles' song "Hey, Jude."

"That's what this is," Sam broke in. "A hopeless cause. So you get your skates back, Gene. So what. There won't be anywhere to skate anyway."

"Well, pretty soon the weather'll be too bad to skate the Stairs, so it won't matter." I wondered why I felt I needed to get their permission.

"Gene needs to get his Shimas back in time to win the street comp." Andy put his arm around Corinne. Her purse bumped between their butts then stopped.

Corinne pulled away from Andy. "Win?" She was incredulous. "What about me?" I smiled to myself.

"Well, yeah, you know." He was so lame. She was gonna eat him alive. "Gene's really good."

"You don't think I'm good?" Corinne demanded.

"I didn't think you were really gonna enter," Andy said. "I figured we'd watch together."

"Watch?" Corinne was so pissed off she seemed like she might start whacking him with her purse like a little old lady.

"Yeah, watch Gene," Andy said, once again convincing me that love must lower your IQ more than a few points.

"It's not like girls do street comps," Sam explained.

"Why not?" Corinne glared at Andy, even though he wasn't the one who said it.

"Because guys don't want to lose," I blurted out.

"Hah!" Corinne laughed. Sam and Brady looked at me like I was a traitor. Andy looked worried like he was losing ground on some cosmic Corinne rating system. Andy minus ten. Gene, he hit! he scored!—plus one hundred.

"I want to get my skates back," I said. "But you probably don't want me to," I told Corinne. "You're afraid of the competition."

"Right. Like I'd have to worry about a loser like you."

"Just build the damn fence and get your skates back," Brady said.

"Yeah, build the fence," Corinne said. "Waste your time while I'm practicing."

"Lost cause," Brady pointed out. He belted out the chorus from "Hey, Jude." His black cloud of hair floated over him as he sang.

Corinne hit him with her purse and the rest of us joined in, nah-nahing at the top of our lungs.

I was still singing to myself when I dumped my stuff inside the front door and headed to the kitchen to make a sandwich. Yellow trotted after me with his sloppy open-mouthed grin. I didn't even have to look at him. I could hear how happy he was—pant, pant, pant. I could smell his dog-breath smile.

"You are so lucky," I told him. "You don't have to go to school. You don't have to do homework. You don't have to work for whacked-out nuns and their lost causes." He grinned at me in agreement and rooted around the floor for crumbs.

As I headed out to do my penance for the evil Sister Jude, I felt relieved that at least my friends wouldn't hate me too much. Maybe I could do a bad job. A fence that looked good enough to get my skates back, then collapsed the minute I skated by.

When I got there, Billy was pounding stakes into the ground. I said hi to him, stood there like an idiot watching him and finally asked, "Uh, is there something you want me to do?"

He just kept working, measuring things, squinting as he stood back and tried to visualize how something would look. He dropped a stake and it rolled down the hill so I scrambled after it and handed it back to him. "Anything I can do to help?" I asked. He just kept working.

You're forcing yourself to help this crazy guy build a fence and he doesn't even take advantage of your help. So you find yourself standing there miserably doing nothing when you could be home enjoying yourself doing nothing. What do you do?

A. Stand there like an idiot because at least you're keeping your part of the bargain.
B. Butt in, grab a hammer, and say, "Hey, buddy, maybe there's a reason you live out of a shopping cart in the woods. You need help big time."
C. Get out of there as fast as you can even if it means you'll never see your skates again.

I started to cut out but, of course, the voice of God, well she acted like she was God, boomed out from the doors. "Eugene, why aren't you helping Billy?"

"He won't let me."

"Billy, why won't you let Eugene help you?"

"I'm busy," Billy said.

"He's supposed to help you so you'd better find something for him to do," Sister Jude boomed. "And you'd better help him," she lectured me.

Billy rolled his eyes as she disappeared behind the big wood doors. "Sometimes she's such a pain in the ass."

"Do you want me to tie the string to these stakes?" I asked.

"Sure," he said and we spent at least a few minutes silently working side by side. "Now I need to figure out where we can get the wood," he said when we finished.

"You don't have any wood?"

"Sister Jude," Billy said, rolling his eyes again. "Tells me God will provide."

"When is God supposed to provide this wood?" I asked. "I need to get my skates back."

"I have some friends who might be able to steal some for me."

"What would Sister Jude say to that?" I asked.

"She knows better than to ask questions." Billy smiled. His teeth were still rotten and horrible, but he didn't seem to smell as bad as before. He looked cleaned up. His skin, which had been the color of cigarette ash, was a little less gray and his straggly hair was combed back in a ponytail.

"My dad might have some." The offer slipped out of my mouth before my disengaged brain could put up a barrier. No wood, no fence, I told myself. No fence, no work. This was sounding better and better. Then I reminded myself, no work, no skates.

"What kind of wood?" Dad asked at supper. "How much do you need?"

"Fence wood," I said. "Enough to make a fence."

"A fence!"

"Gene, eat your peas," Mom interrupted.

"I hate peas. You know I hate peas and yet you continue to serve them to me. Do you hate me?"

"Yes." Lily opened her mouth full of green chewed-up stuff.

"Lily." Mom frowned at her.

"You know wood's expensive," Dad said. "How big of a fence are we talking about here?"

"Umm, big enough to go around the stairs at the convent."

"You're building a fence around the Stairs?" Mom sounded surprised. "Does this have to do with that letter we got from the sisters?"

"Yeah, I guess so," I said, digging myself in deeper. "I'm kind of helping them build this fence to keep skaters off the Stairs."

"Aren't your friends mad at you?" Lily asked.

"No, my friends aren't mad at me." I glared at her. "Aren't you done eating? Shouldn't you ask to be excused?"

"I like to listen." She picked up a stray pea that had rolled off her plate and popped it in her mouth just to emphasize who was the good child. "Maybe you need to get a job so you can buy some wood," she suggested.

"So you're volunteering to help the nuns." Mom was just sappy enough to help me get what I needed. "Good for you, Gene."

"A fence around those stairs?" Dad narrowed his eyes. "Is that really necessary? Sounds like an eyesore."

"The design's pretty cool," I said.

"Did one of the nuns design it?" Lily asked.

"No, this guy named Billy." I told her.

"Where's he from?" Mom asked.

"Uh, he lives by the river."

"On Seabury Avenue?" Dad named the street where rich people lived in our neighborhood. "What's his last name? Maybe I know him."

"I don't know his last name," I admitted. "He's kind of a bum."

"There are all these homeless people that hang out at the convent now," Lily announced. "I heard Shannon's mom complaining about them."

"You know, I've heard there's been an increase in vandalism recently," Mom said.

"I've noticed some guys in pretty bad shape walking around the neighborhood," Dad said. "I wondered what was going on."

"Billy's okay. Please, Dad, I need to help him build the fence."

"I've got some scraps out in the garage you can use," Dad said.

"Thanks, Dad." I got up and cleared my plate before he changed his mind.

"Although I'm not sure I want to be contributing to a neighborhood eyesore," he added. I grabbed my skates and headed out so I didn't have to hear the rest.

I skated over to Andy's and rang his front bell. The door opened, and Corinne was standing there like she owned the place. "Sorry, wrong house," I said, "I was looking for your Siamese twin. You know, the one you're attached at the butt to?"

"Funny." She sounded sarcastic but I could tell she was trying hard not to smile.

"He was going to help me practice for the competition," I explained.

"He's busy." Corinne stood there like she was trying to make up her mind about something. "I can help you," she offered.

"You'd help the competition?" I asked. I felt myself turning red because I was thinking, you'd hang out with me instead of Andy?

"You need help." Corinne shook her head at me like I was a sorry specimen of a skater. "Besides, I really don't care about this one. So you win a few bucks. I'm waiting for the big one in the spring so I can get hooked up with a skate company."

This sounded like such a good idea, I almost decided I'd wait until spring too. Then I remember Corinne wanted to help me.

She'd disappeared into the house, and I started to follow her when I heard her yell, "Hey, Andy, I've got to go home now."

Now I was really confused. Maybe she wasn't going to hang out with me after all.

"Shh," Corinne put her finger to her lips as she walked toward me. "I'm not going to be responsible for him not acing his chemistry test," she whispered. "Let's get out of here before he decides to blow off studying and come with us."

"Okay."

Once we were outside, Corrine said, "We've got to go to my house and get my skates."

"Okay." I followed her as slowly as I could in skates, trying not to give off happy vibes, like I was a big goofy dog. Or Andy.

We went a few blocks to a dead-end street I'd never noticed before. She turned at this grandma house that had a yard populated by lawn gnomes. I stopped at the door, but she motioned me inside.

As I bent over and tried to pull my skates off without breaking one of the five million china knickknacks that were everywhere, an old lady, not much bigger than one of the lawn gnomes, came in the room.

"It's your boyfriend again," she said to Corinne.

"No, Grandma," Corinne said in a loud voice. Either the old lady was hard of hearing, or Corinne wanted to make sure I heard this. "Andy's my boyfriend. This is Gene."

"Oh." Corinne's grandma frowned. "I like this one better. He's taking his shoes off. He has better manners."

"Skates, Grandma," Corinne enunciated. "If Andy had skates on he would have taken them off."

Corinne's grandma walked over and looked me up and down. "You're right, dear, the other one had better manners. This one won't even talk to me."

I looked at Corinne like what was I supposed to say.

"Gene. That must be short for Eugene. A lovely name."

"Mom?" Corinne yelled up the stairs. "Are you going to class?"

"In a minute," her mom yelled back.

We went upstairs to this pink frilly room that reminded me of Lily's Barbie dream house. "We're living with my grandma until my mom finishes school," Corinne explained. She opened the closet door and a pile of black clothes spilled across the floor. She dug around and pulled out her skates.

"Mom, can we ride with you to the U?" she said when her mom, who looked like the only normal person in this place, appeared.

I decided to show Corinne that my manners weren't that bad, by making polite conversation with her mother in the car. "What are you majoring in Mrs. Camden?" I asked.

"Wiznowski," she corrected. "I just changed back to my maiden name." She sighed and didn't answer my question.

"Oh," I said.

"Gene's dad is an artist," Corinne told her.

"Really." Ms. Wiznowski's beaten-down voice got some energy.

"Yeah." I started to tell her what he did but she interrupted.

"It must be wonderful to make money doing something you love," she said, like she was studying something miserable like being a prison guard or a substitute teacher.

"Yeah, I guess so." I didn't mention that it's not like my dad floated around all happy most of the time. He was usually making snide comments and complaining about how he had too much work to do.

Corinne's mom dropped us off and said to keep track of the time because she'd be back in an hour and a half. I planned to work on basics. Chris Edwards said you had to know the fundamentals first and build on them. And I figured that way I wouldn't embarrass myself in front of Corinne.

"Let's work on your blindside half cab soul," Corinne said, like she'd been planning this ever since she first saw me wipe out at the Stairs.

"Right." This sounded like about as much fun as Corinne's mom was having.

"Hey, I can help you with this if you'll let me."

I skated backwards toward the ledge at Nollie Ollie and missed it.

"You're not coming at the right angle," Corinne instructed. "Watch me and see how I turn myself so I don't lose sight of it." She turned her back toward the ledge but managed to hit it perfectly. She had this tough, athletic way of doing things. She skated like she talked.

I tried again but blew it. She shook her head. "You're not watching me close enough."

I snorted. She had no idea how wrong she was. "I wish I had my video camera," I told her. "Then I could see you in slow motion, freeze frame you to figure out what you're doing."

"I'll do it in slow motion." She was such a hot dog. She did these exaggerated movements back to the ledge, turned her hips and stepped up. "Now you do it," she ordered.

I slow motioned it backwards, then scrambled up the ledge and collapsed. She started laughing, skated up and collapsed next to me. "Were you watching my head at all to see when I turned it?"

"No," I admitted, not mentioning I was distracted by some other body parts.

"Stand up," she said. And as we stood, she grabbed my face. "Turn here so you can see the ledge." She turned my head.

"Oh." My face was in her hands, inches from hers.

"Oh," she said and got this look that made me think maybe I was supposed to kiss her. I leaned towards her and she dropped her hands and turned away. "I wonder if Andy's done with his chemistry. I'd better have my mom drop me off at his house."

"Oh, yeah, Andy," I said, thinking, *Gene, you are such an idiot.* I skated away and did a pissed off blindside half cab soul. Turning my head, following directions like the good guy I was, and so what, nailed it.

CHAPTER EIGHT
GETTING A LIFE

"You raise an interesting point, Mr. Martin," Mr. Mac said in response to Derek's whining, as usual, about how the Democrats' commercials were unfair to Republicans.

"What a dickhead," I mouthed to Andy, shaking my head at Derek. It killed me how Mr. Mac let him go on and on, actually encouraging him. Sometimes I hated how Mr. Mac seemed to be above it all. I wished he'd just come out and tell us who he was going to vote for. Mr. Mac pulled out a pile of handouts from his never-ending supply, dealing them to us like a deck of cards. "Read these and the next chapter in your book for tomorrow. Oh, and bring in a one-page typed response to the readings."

"Leave it to Mr. Mac to suck the fun out of everything," Corinne complained on our way to second hour.

"Yeah." I was grateful Corinne was treating me same as usual. Maybe what had happened the other night was totally in my mind. "I just want one sign from Mr. Mac that we're right, Derek Martin's wrong, and he's voting for Wellstone," I said. I'd been hanging around Sister Jude too much. I wanted to convert Mr. Mac to my righteous cause.

It was hard not to feel poor and oppressed, yourself, when you had to listen to Sister Jude's ongoing monologue about the poor and oppressed. I'd almost walked away from this stupid fence-building project. Except that every once in a while when Sister Jude left, Billy talked to me and I couldn't help but wonder about him.

That afternoon, I headed over to the Stairs. I didn't see Billy so I went to Sister Jude's office. She was on her ancient phone with what must have been the one person in the world who talked more than she did. She went, "uh huh . . . I see . . . why yes . . . uh huh . . ." as she motioned me inside. As I stood there waiting, I noticed a picture in the middle of the crowd of angels on her shelf. It was a photo of Sister Jude, a bunch of scraggly men and a guy with a big grin on his face. When Sister Jude finally got off the phone, I blurted out, "Do you know Paul Wellstone?"

"I should hope so," she said. "Why?"

"That picture." I pointed to the shelf. "Isn't that you and Paul Wellstone?"

"Of course I know Paul. He's one of my angels, honey."

I waited for her to go on, expecting her usual self righteous sermon: Paul Wellstone, unlike you, you privileged kid, is a friend to the oppressed and downtrodden, giving me the details about how she met him at some protest where they were protesting people like me. But she just sat there staring at me with her unblinking eyes and this satisfied smile. I didn't have a clue what I was supposed to do. So I backed out the office door and took off down the hall in search of Billy again.

I found him at the Stairs, sawing away like he'd been there all along. It was strange, he was so full of nervous energy that I didn't expect him to be safe around sharp objects, but building things seems to calm his rabbity nervousness.

"Say, Billy," I asked, helping him move some boards over to the sawhorses. "How does Sister Jude know Paul Wellstone?"

"Vets," Billy said.

"I'm a vet," Billy said, after we sawed and piled enough boards for one side of the fence.

"Oh. Were you in Vietnam?"

He nodded and grunted. One of the nuns came out with lemonade for us. "Thanks," I said.

"It's leftover from last night's Loaves and Fishes," she said, like she wanted to make sure I knew she wouldn't do anything as wasteful and luxurious as make lemonade just for us. "Our meal program for the poor."

"Oh." This must have been why, all of the sudden, there were all these bums coming up from the river and from the liquor store on Franklin Avenue.

"Poor people have to eat too," Billy said.

"They do?" I asked sarcastically. I was sick of him and Sister Jude treating me like I was some sheltered rich kid who didn't know anything.

"So do you know Paul Wellstone?" Sister Jude snuck up on us, as usual.

"Uh, yeah."

"Good," she said, like maybe I wasn't as hopeless as she'd thought.

I made it home before my friends appeared to watch our progress from across the street. It made me nervous because I was afraid Billy might lose it or Sister Jude would come out and start a shouting match. It was like we were putting on this weird play and my friends were the audience. And God knows Sister Jude liked an audience.

At supper, Dad went on and on about Paul Wellstone's vote against the Iraq War resolution, the resolution to give President Bush authority to attack Iraq without the rest of the world's support. "I can't believe it," he said. "He's still ahead in the polls. People like it that he had the guts to do what he believed was right even though it could cost him the election."

"Of course," Mom said because she, like all teachers and mothers, believed if you do the right thing you'll be rewarded.

"I knew he'd vote against it," I said. "I told him supporting Bush on Iraq was bull . . . uh b.s."

"What?" Mom struggled between the good news I'd talked to Paul Wellstone about something important and the bad news I used language that didn't have the kindergarten seal of approval.

"I didn't mean to," I tried to explain. "He was just so easy to talk to. It kind of popped out."

Mom shook her head but decided not to lecture me. "We're going to a Wellstone fundraiser this weekend. You can congratulate him and have him sign your book."

"But Mom," I complained. "This might be one of the last good skating weekends before winter. And I'm training for the street competition."

"It's not like it'll last all weekend. Just an hour or so Saturday afternoon," Dad said. "Right?" He gave Mom a worried look like what had she gotten us into this time.

"I'll go," said Lily.

"Of course you'll go," I said. "Let's face it, you don't have a life."

"I do so!" Lily screwed up her face like she was about to cry, and Mom shook her head at me.

I shrugged. "Hey, it's not my fault if she can't handle the truth."

Of course, this made Mom bound and determined that I shouldn't have a life too. And so I found myself standing in line for an entire Saturday afternoon to shake hands for two seconds with Paul Wellstone.

I tried to leave his book at home but Mom made me go back and get it. I started reading it but didn't finish. And I didn't want him asking me about it because he wasn't the kind of person you could lie to, and somehow it seemed important not to let him down.

I drummed the book against my leg to relieve my boredom. This got Dad's attention.

"So you haven't made a dent in my wood pile yet."

"Billy got some other wood."

"Well, that's probably for the best," Dad said. "A fence made from my scrap pile would have been a taste crime."

"Yeah." I didn't mention that instead this fence was just a plain old crime. The wood was so nice, I was pretty sure it was stolen.

"I keep meaning to come over and check it out," Dad said. "I'd like to meet this Billy." Mom was all proud of me because I was helping the nuns, and it occurred to me Dad was just as proud because I was building something.

It also occurred to me that Dad and Billy meeting each other would be so awkward I couldn't let it happen. I could see Dad trying to make conversation with Billy and Billy just staring at him. It was like I was leading this double life. I could see the tabloid headlines: "Fifteen-year-old boy lives secret life among the nuns and bums. 'I've become a carpenter,' he said, 'just like Jesus.'"

"Uh, Billy's really shy, Dad. It might make him too self-conscious to work."

"Oh." He sounded disappointed. "How about if I just walk by when you're not working?"

"Do you have to?"

"Gene." Mom was eavesdropping. "It's his neighborhood too. He has the right to check out projects going on in his own neighborhood. I've checked it out."

"You have?"

"I have too," said Lily. "We met that sister lady."

I groaned.

"What's wrong with that?" Mom demanded. "She's seems very nice."

"Oh, not Sister Jude then."

"No, that's her name. You don't think she's nice?"

"Not really," I snorted.

"She said you are a lovely boy." Mom knew how to totally humiliate me.

"She said you're pretty," Lily giggled.

"Shut up, you wiener."

"Mo-oom!"

She was lucky Mom wouldn't let me call her anything worse than wiener. I thought of it as kindergarten code for dickhead.

"Such a lovely boy, such lovely children." Dad's voice dripped with sarcasm.

Mom changed the subject. "Let's talk about the family reunion. You guys are going to love this camp we found. It's just outside of Eveleth. Camp Chicagami."

"Camp Chicky Monkey," Dad teased.

I sighed. Not only did I have to waste this totally great afternoon, but I had to waste it planning how to ruin my summer. The line moved a couple of centimeters. Just enough for us to see the crowd in front of us around the corner. "Mom," I said, "I don't know how much longer I can wait. I promised Andy I'd meet him at Nollie Ollie at two."

"I want to give Paul my picture," Lily whined. Her latest masterpiece was a drawing of Paul Wellstone under a giant rainbow. Mom told her he'd love it because he used to head this political group called the Rainbow Coalition. I tried to point out that all little girls drew dumb rainbows, but Mom insisted on acting like it was this original work of genius.

"Don't you want him to sign your book?" Mom asked.

"Not really." It wasn't that I didn't want him to sign it. I wanted to be able to say I'd read it and impress him with my insights.

"Not really," Mom repeated. She shook her head like she couldn't believe it.

"Hey," Dad interrupted. "We're about there."

So finally, I found myself standing in front of Paul Wellstone, bracing myself to listen to him tell me how disappointed he was that I couldn't finish his skimpy little book. Or worse yet, that he didn't remember who I was.

"Gene!" He about shook my hand off. "You were right."

"Yeah." I shrugged.

My parents looked back and forth between me and Paul Wellstone.

"Gene said he wouldn't vote for me if I supported Bush on Iraq," Paul Wellstone explained. "Of course, I was convinced that when I voted against the Iraq Resolution, no one would vote for me. But what else could I do?"

"You did the only thing you could do," Mom, the do-gooder agreed.

"I kept seeing your son's face and the faces of all of these other young people I've talked to over the years and I couldn't justify putting them at risk just so I could win an election. Besides, I think people want you to do what you think is right."

Dad nodded. Even he couldn't stay cynical in the hopeful presence of Paul Wellstone.

"I brought my book."

"Great! I'd love to sign it." He pulled out a pen.

"You got into a lot of trouble," I said, because I felt like I should say something, even if it was lame.

"I still get into a lot of trouble." He laughed, then screwed up his face as he concentrated on writing.

"Thanks." I took the book back and forced myself to appear cool by not looking to see what he wrote.

"Thanks for your vote," he said. "With your help we can win, Gene."

This time it didn't even bother me that I couldn't vote, that there wasn't a whole lot I could do to help him win. It was like he was talking about something bigger than this election. Maybe that was how he always won.

"What did he write?" Mom asked when we got in the car.

"Just a second," I said, as Lily tried to grab the book away from me. "Gene—Always do what you think is right (even if it gets you in trouble)—Paul," I read.

"Wow," Lily said. "He's telling you to get in trouble."

"Sometimes that's okay," Mom said. "If it's for the right cause," she explained.

"Wow," I echoed Lily. Only Paul Wellstone could have gotten my mom, the kindergarten teacher, to say something like that.

Dad dropped me off at Nollie Ollie. Andy was waiting for me looking bored out of his skull. "What took you so long?"

"My mom." I didn't want to admit I was glad I spent the day waiting for Paul Wellstone.

"Can't you do something about her? Like tell her to get a life and leave yours alone?"

"Right. Maybe you should talk to her." Maybe Andy should've talked to her. We took the PSAT on Wednesday, stuck for hours in the creaky seats in the auditorium. My mom made me study so much I was bored before I started. Andy, of course, didn't study at all but, that wouldn't stop him from being a National Merit scholar.

Andy got up from the grass where he was lounging and stretched in slow motion. For somebody who could hardly wait for me to come, he was sure taking his time getting going. "You think I should talk to her?" He started spazzing all over the place in outrage. "I'm afraid of her."

"What—are you afraid she'll make you sit in the time-out chair?"

Andy fake shivered. "The time-out chair. I forgot about that. You know Brady used to tell me it was really an electric chair, and if you didn't sit totally still she'd zap you."

"Oh, yeah, that's true," I said. "She showed me once where the switch was."

Andy, with his warped imagination, got into this. "Wouldn't that be a great invention? What if you could wire chairs in class so if some douchebag like Derek Martin wouldn't shut up, you could fry him." He started spazzing like someone who was being electrocuted, jerking his arms and legs and ending up on the ground again.

I had my skates on by then and skated away in disgust at how he was wasting my time.

"Hey wait!" He came after me on his board. "Seriously, I'm afraid of your mom. I'm afraid she'll turn her niceness beam on me. There's nothing more painful than having her look at you with that look, you know, that look like she knows you're one bludgeon away from being a mass murderer but she's going to save you. And then the way her voice gets . . ." He got all syrupy: "'Now, Andrew, I know you didn't really mean to hit

74

Tiffany over the head with that weapon you made of Lincoln Logs. Why don't you and Tiffany go to the dress-up area and play dolls together?' You know your mother spent that entire year trying to turn me into a transvestite. And it probably would've worked if Tiffany Peterson wasn't always crying and getting snot on all the dresses."

I did about three half spins during Andy's tirade. I had enough speed going I whirred like a Tasmanian devil. What Andy said about my mom was true. Why did she have to be on this mission to find the goodness in everybody? Why did she have to be so sickening? Then it occurred to me that was why she hit it off with Sister Jude. They were a lot alike. It was like my mom was the white witch and Sister Jude was the black. "Ouch!" I rammed into a wall.

"Gene, I've got some bad news." Andy skated up to me.

"Am I bleeding?" My nose felt like a piece of cheese that had been run across a grater.

"Not really. You've just got a pattern on your face."

"Great." I started to skate again.

Andy followed me. "I'm not going to be able to skip school next Friday to help you practice. My mom's down on me for skipping sixth hour so much and—"

"But that's gym. Why don't you tell *your* mom to get a life?" Andy was the one who talked me into doing this stupid street competition, and he was ditching me. "If I don't skip school, I won't get enough practice in."

"I just can't risk it," Andy finished lamely. "Sorry."

"Sorry?" I started circling around him, skating faster and faster. Then I stopped. "What am I supposed to do? Go by myself? I don't even have decent skates. I can't believe you got me into this." I started skating really fast and hard again.

Andy got all mopey and pathetic and skated toward me. "Since I can't do it, I asked Corinne."

I stopped dead in my tracks. "Corinne?"

"Yeah, you're right." He shook his shaggy head. "It was a dumb idea."

"No, no . . ." I jumped in before he changed his mind. "It's a lot better than nothing. She's pretty good at teaching stuff." I felt myself turn red at the memory of her face next to mine.

"Not as good as me though, right?"

"Oh, no, Not as good as you." Andy never really taught me anything. He just hung out for moral support and watched for cops.

"Corinne's mom is too depressed about her own life to care if she skips school," Andy explained.

"Yeah," I agreed. Who wouldn't be depressed living in that gnome house with that weird little old lady? "I hope my mom doesn't kill me." I'd never skipped a whole day of school before.

"It'll be worth it." Andy was relieved I was going along with his plan.

"Yeah." Corinne agreed to skip school to spend the whole day with me. I did a perfect blindside half cab soul, just how Corinne taught me.

"Nice," said Andy.

CHAPTER NINE

WIENER

When Friday finally came, I was up early, dressed and eating a bowl of weird health-food Cheerios that I had to dump a ton of sugar on.

Lily tried to grab the comics from me. "Go back to bed," she ordered.

"I have to get going early today. I have a project."

"What's your project?" Mom sat down and gave me her full unwanted attention.

"It's a group thing, we've hardly started," I said, coldly, hoping to convey the message that, if she asked me anything else, I'd never talk to her again.

"Oh," Mom said in this hurt voice. "I'd like to hear about it when you're done."

Lily tried to pull the comics from me again, but I held on to them and we were in a tug of war. "Look, jerk face, I could've read them by now if you weren't such a wiener. Besides you can hardly read."

"I can so!" She yanked so hard they ripped, and she almost fell off her chair. Then she started fake crying, one of her tricks Mom always fell for.

Just then Dad, who was totally oblivious to us, looked up from the front page and said in this amazed, happy voice, "We're gonna win!"

"What? The war?" Lily miraculously stopped crying.

"There is no war." I rolled my eyes at her. "Yet."

Dad shook his head. "Paul. He's maintaining his lead."

"You need to be more of an optimist, Ray," Mom said.

"You're right. If Paul pulls this off, I'm changing my ways and becoming an optimist."

"If?" Mom was incredulous. "If?"

"You're right, Kathy." Dad grinned. "I am now officially an optimist."

Just then Corinne showed up at our back door. I grabbed my stuff and went before my mom asked her about our nonexistent group project. I figured I could sneak out while my family was momentarily distracted by Dad's sudden personality change.

"Hey, are you embarrassed by me?" Corinne asked as I walked fast past her and around the house.

"I figured you didn't want to be interrogated." I kept walking till we reached the end of the block where I stopped to put on my skates.

"You think I'd tell your mom we're skipping school," she accused.

"You wouldn't mean to. But you don't know my mom. She's tricky. She'd trip you up."

"How?" Corinne demanded. "How could someone's clueless mom get me to say anything about bailing out of school?"

"Well." I turned to Corinne who was dressed in her baggy skate pants and a T-shirt that actually fit instead of being ten sizes too small. I said in a sappy mom voice, "It's so nice to see a girl wearing comfortable clothes to school these days." Then I returned to my normal voice, "And you wouldn't be able to stop yourself. You'd say, 'I wouldn't be caught dead wearing these to school. These are my skate clothes.'"

"Would not!" She shoved me.

"Would so." I shoved her back. "Definitely." I felt like I was play fighting with Lily, but I wanted it to go on forever.

"Where should we go first?" Corinne was all business.

"How about Minnehaha Falls?" I felt superior because I knew what was nearby. "It's a big park with a lot of concrete and hardly any people on weekdays."

"Great!" Then she got all enthusiastic about skating, which made me wonder if that's all this day was to her.

We took off, skating past the Stairs which were almost fenced in but not done in time for me to get my skates back for the competition. I tried to get Sister Jude to cut me some slack and give them to me a couple of days early, but all she did was give me a lecture about the youth of today and the value of deferred gratification.

It wasn't the greatest weather, but at least it wasn't raining. Every once in a while the sun came out as we skated down River Road, and I watched it glint on Corinne's hair when I dropped behind her. Why did girls have hair like that? Boys' hair was just hair, but Corinne's hair looked so soft and full of light it made you want to touch it.

"What are you doing back there?" Corinne interrupted my thoughts.

"Skating. What are you doing?" Like I would've wanted her to know she was turning me into someone who could do voice-overs for shampoo commercials.

When we reached Minnehaha Falls, it was deserted except for these enormous trees that seemed to be watching us. We skated the ramp on the bandshell and the curved rail by the waterfall. Corinne was less than impressed until we left the park and found this killer hand rail by the river.

"Wow," she said. "You take your suicide skating seriously."

"This isn't so bad. I hear there's one in the suburbs that makes this look like a kiddie ride."

She pulled off her T-shirt and stood there in this skimpy beater, looking macho and undeniably female at the same time. I didn't know if it was from looking at Corinne or the rail of death, but my heart started beating really loud. It was like there was a car with the bass turned up parked next to my eardrums.

"Do you want to go first or should I?" She smiled like she was daring me.

I smiled back. "I hate to be rude. But talent oops, I mean age, before beauty."

"Go right ahead, you talented geezer." She gestured to the rail. I'm not sure if she was smiling because I was dumb enough to skate to my doom or if she liked being called beautiful.

I made it about halfway down before I jumped off. I expected Corinne to at least yell down to ask me if I was okay, but instead she said, "Gene, get your butt out of the way. It's my turn."

I scrambled to the side and watched her go down. She was so good. She made the impossible look easy. She made it almost the whole way, then wiped out.

"Okay," I said. "I take it back—you're the talented one."

She clomped up to where I was sitting. "I guess that means you're beautiful."

"That's me," I said. "No talent. I just rely on my good looks." She did like it that I called her beautiful. "Corinne, why aren't you competing? You're better than I am. You skate like Louie Zamora." There—I admitted it.

"Louie Zamora." She looked pleased with herself. She was sitting close enough to me I could see the goose bumps on her bare arm. "You're every bit as good as me. You skate like Dre Powell."

"Who?"

"He skates so pretty. I like watching him move." She turned red and looked away.

"Why aren't you competing?" I went back to the original safe subject. But I memorized the name: Dre Powell.

"It's too late to sign up—isn't it?" We both started clomping up the steps.

"You don't have to sign up. You just show up at the first site and put your ten bucks in the pot."

"Andy didn't tell me that." She sounded hurt instead of mad. "I think he doesn't want me to compete against you."

"That's crazy," I told her as we got to the top and she grabbed her shirt and put it back on.

"It's true. He's like really protective of you, you know. He made a big deal about how I had to help you. I mean not that I didn't want to help you." She turned red again. "I mean, if I was competing against you, I'd be pretty stupid to help you, wouldn't I?"

"Well, I could not enter and help you."

She shook her head. "Yeah. And Andy and everybody would be totally pissed at me."

"Why don't we both enter then? There'll be tons of people competing. It's not like it's just you against me."

"Then why does it feel like that?"

"Because we're the only ones in our group who are good enough," I told her. "Believe me we're not the only ones good enough in the Cities. There are tons of good skaters. I got close last year but I didn't win."

"I've never helped somebody try to beat me."

81

"Just think," I said. "If either of us wins, then you automatically win because you'd be partly responsible for the other person winning."

"Oh, yeah?" Corinne was getting ready to do the rail again.

"Yeah. Now tell me your secret. How do you stay on so long?"

"I take a deep breath before I start and I exhale it down," she said. "My breath just pulls me in the right direction."

I watched her grind even further and with more stability than the time before. Then she stood at the bottom waiting for me like she thought I was really going to make it that far.

I took a deep breath and started. But I wiped out right away. "I don't think that breath thing works for me," I yelled down.

She stood directly at the bottom of the path and yelled back, "If you're pissed at me, imagine yourself heading right towards me so you can knock me down. Don't worry. If you get to the end, I'll jump out of the way."

"If you say so." I wasn't really pissed at her. So I didn't try to run her down. Instead, I imagined skating straight towards her, imagined her not moving but opening her arms. I shot down like an arrow.

Corinne jumped out of the way at the last minute. "That was fantastic! Okay, now you can teach me. What's your secret?"

"I'll never tell," I said. And she laughed like I was joking.

By mid afternoon, we'd checked out a bunch of other places and grabbed lunch at McDonald's. I felt like I was one of those little transformer guys you get in a Happy Meal: I'd changed. I moved to a whole new level of expertise even with those crappy skates. And Corinne and I were different together.

We weren't fighting or painfully uncomfortable. We were friends. I still had this barely controllable urge to touch her but it was okay, I was happy just being with her.

We skated back along the river, the last leaves of October falling around us. Corinne went on and on about skate techniques, talking my ear off like I was the only person in the world who spoke her language. When we reached my house, she smiled her crooked-mouth smile at me. It made me want to skate toward her again but I just said, "Thanks. You really helped me."

"You know it really is okay," she said, "if we both enter tomorrow. I mean, I'd be totally cool with either of us winning."

"Yeah," I agreed. "I'm glad you're gonna do it."

She smiled again and skated away. I stood there watching her skate down the sidewalk under the falling leaves and thought about how for once in my life, I didn't need to consider the options. I could bask in the effects of my awesomely good choices. It was like I told Lily the other day when she called me a wiener: "You don't know the English language very well. I'm not a wiener. I'm a winner."

I opened the door, just at the time when I should have been coming home from school. I was going to pull this off—yes! Yellow didn't come to meet me, which was strange. I walked into the living room and there he was sitting at Dad's feet. It was so weird—Dad was on the couch crying.

Chapter Ten

Give Peace a Chance

I'd never seen Dad cry before. I didn't know what to do. "Dad," I asked, "are you okay?"

"Sure," he said, "I'll be okay." Then he started crying again and just sat there like he expected me to say something.

"Um, Dad, I've got to do some homework."

I headed up to my bedroom as he asked, "What are we going to do now, Gene?"

Something bad had happened, and he thought I knew about it. I grabbed my cell and called Andy. "Did something bad happen while I was gone? Are my mom and sister okay?"

"Are you kidding?" he said. "Don't you know what happened?"

"No! Tell me. Would you tell me what happened?"

"It's Wellstone," Andy said. "His plane went down."

"What?"

"He's dead, Gene. His wife, his daughter, everybody on the plane."

"Dead? But I just talked to him . . ."

Andy started going on and on about how all they did in school all day was watch the news. "It was a good day to skip."

"Right." I collapsed on my bed numb, not listening anymore. I stayed there not able to think of anything at all. I stayed there until it was dark and Mom called me for supper.

Supper was bad. Not the food. Mom made spaghetti, which was what she did when she kind of forgot about supper until the last minute. Lily kept going on and on about how her teacher cried in front of the whole class and some kid gave her a Kleenex, which made her cry even harder.

"That sounds like my class." Mom looked terrible. Her face was pale and puffy. "It was a hard day to be a teacher. All I wanted was for somebody to make it better, and it's always supposed to be me . . ." She looked like she was going to cry, then stopped herself. "What was it like at South, Gene?"

And I said, "I don't know," because, let's face it, I didn't. Then I remembered what Andy said. "We watched the news all day."

Dad didn't say much. Yellow sat under the table groaning like an old walrus. "What's the matter with him?" I asked.

"He knows we're sad," Lily said.

"He is an expressive animal," Dad said. Yellow poked his face up and put his smelly dog breath head on Dad's lap. "An unappetizing, yet expressive, animal." Dad finally started eating, and Lily giggled.

Things seemed back to normal until Mom announced we were going to the state Capitol to a vigil that night.

"What's that?" Lily asked.

"We light candles to honor Paul and Sheila and the other people who died," Mom told her.

"Like a backwards birthday party," Lily said.

Dad teared up, and Mom put her hand on his shoulder. Was he just going to keep crying in front of us like he didn't care at all that we'd never seen him cry? "Umm, I've got plans," I said.

"What kind of plans?" Mom demanded.

"Umm . . ." Anything but standing around watching a bunch of grown men cry while their wives patted their backs.

Just then the phone rang. I got up to answer it, but Mom told me to let it go to the answering machine.

I realized too late who was calling. "This is the South High attendance office on Friday, the 25th of October," the recording announced. "Notifying you that Eugene Snow had an unexcused absence for the entire day."

Your mom and dad and your dutifully shocked little sister have caught you skipping an entire day of school, not just health class or Spanish when there's a sub and everyone sleeps through a dubbed-in Spanish version of *El Mermaid Pequena,* but the whole honking day of school. And somehow your skipping school and Paul Wellstone's plane crashing have become stuck together with crazy glue, and you don't know how to get them apart. What do you do?

A. Say a mistake was made, because, let's face it, one was, and hope that they buy it was the attendance office, not you, that blew it big time.
B. Plead your case about needing to practice for the skate comp which is your future career, so it's kind of related to higher education.
C. Leave the table because at the moment, everything seems to matter too much and not matter anymore.

I got up from the table and mumbled, "Can I be excused," without waiting for an answer. I shut myself in my bedroom and nobody followed and knocked on my door. Nobody came and told me I had to come with them to the vigil, that we needed to discuss this. Instead, I heard them leave. I heard them come back. I stayed shut in my room sketching cartoon monsters, wadding them up and throwing them across the room at the garbage can. I tried calling Andy. No answer. I went online, but it was a bunch of assholes I had no desire to talk to. Paul Wellstone looked up at me from the cover of his book on the floor. "People want you to do what you think is right," I heard him say. "Shut up," I told him. "Just shut up and leave me alone."

The next morning, Mom appeared at my door. "You know, young man, you are in big trouble."

I looked at the clock—it was only 8:30. That sucked. Then I remembered what day it was. The skate competition.

"I'm sorry." I started to plead my case about going to the comp. How I needed her or Dad to hang out in the car so I could drive to each site. But she interrupted me. She gave me a lecture about the importance of school and all this obvious stuff, then dropped the big one.

"I've talked to Corinne's mother and Andy's mom. Andy says that you can get extra credit from Mr. Mac by going to the peace rally in St. Paul today and writing an essay about it. God knows you'll need the extra credit," she said, like I'd skipped class for a month instead of a day.

"But, Mom. The street comp is today."

"They'll manage without you," she said, totally missing the point.

So I found myself getting in the car with my family, Andy, Corinne, and her new best friend, Lark, to go to some boring demonstration. I just hoped Dad could control his emotions until we got there and could skate away. Mom finally asked me why I wasn't wearing my regular skates. I told her they had a bad wheel bearing.

Lark motioned Corinne to get in the middle with Lily between them. Lark annoyed me. Andy and I called her Euro Girl. Not to her face of course. To her face, we pretended to be Belgian boys and call her Lar-kuh. She, of course, didn't get that we were making fun of her. She said we were the only Americans who pronounced her name right and remembered that she was Dutch not French, whatever difference that made. Andy seemed pretty disgusted at being exiled to the far back away from Corinne, so I tried to cheer him up. "Want me to hold your hand?" I said.

"Shut up." He elbowed me.

"What does your shirt say, Andy?" Mom called back from the front seat, trying to make sure everyone felt included.

"Make love not war." Andy looked down at his chest grinning.

"Hmm," said Mom. I imagined the worry lines appearing on her forehead as she considered how Andy's crummy T-shirt would encourage every teenager who saw it to start having sex immediately.

"Don't worry, Mrs. Snow," Lark reassured her. "It's no big deal. You Americans need to get over your sexual hang-ups."

"I bought it because it reminded me of Andy," Corinne bragged. "At Savers."

"I bought Ray a shirt like that years ago." Mom's voice was high, like she was trying to be one of the girls. "Very effective. Remember, Ray?"

"Yeah, especially when I gave it to my dad as a hand-me-down."

"Yuck," I said, moving from the disgusting image of my mom and dad getting all hot and heavy while he was wearing this dumb shirt, to my potbellied grandpa parading in front of my grandma in it.

"He used it as a rag," Dad explained.

"It is refreshing," Lark said, "to meet Americans who are so freewheeling and politically active."

Refreshing? Freewheeling? I wondered where Lark learned English. Probably not from a human.

"Hey, could we get some heat back here?" I asked. It was cold and gray outside like it had turned into winter overnight. Not the greatest day to skate, I consoled myself. "Do you think they cancelled the street comp?" I asked Andy.

"Why?"

"I dunno. Because of the weather." Because I couldn't skate in it. I turned so I could see the backs of the girls' heads. Corinne had a knit cap pulled over her ears. I tried to remember how her hair had looked the day before when the sun came out from behind a cloud. "Corinne." I tried to get her attention but she ignored me.

"I checked online," Andy said. "One of the sites is pretty close to the Capitol."

"Oh, yeah?"

"It's in downtown St. Paul," he lowered his voice. "I thought maybe we could bail out of this peace-and-love fest and check it out."

"Have you talked to the girls?" I asked.

"I told Corinne, but I don't know if she's told Lark."

I groaned. Lark was such a suck up. She'd never go.

"You should talk to her, Gene," Andy whispered. "Corinne says Lark kind of likes you."

"What?"

He laughed and elbowed me.

"What were you saying about the progressive movement, Lark?" Mom continued some conversation that no normal human being under the age of thirty would be caught dead in.

"Mister Wellstone was such a hero to you," Lark announced like she was an anthropologist interpreting our primitive culture. "His movement can't go on without him." I couldn't tell from her accent if she was making a statement or asking a question.

"Yes it can." Mom was using her *Little Engine That Could* voice. "And it will."

"Maybe it can't," Dad said.

"That's a terrible thing to say."

"Someone has to say it," Dad told her.

"Not someone in our family." Mom's voice shook like she was really angry.

I glanced at Andy. He rolled his eyes, and I could tell he was thinking, get me outta here, as soon as possible.

Dad pulled into the Sears parking lot by the state capitol, popped the back hatch, and Andy and I scrambled out. We both wore our old blades.

"Meet us back at the car afterwards," Dad said.

I started off for the Cathedral where the rally was beginning, then turned to find that Andy wasn't behind me. He was waiting for Corinne. Corinne, of course, was waiting for Lark who was trying to put on Corinne's hand-me-down skates in the freezing cold. It was obvious she'd never worn a pair of skates in her life. After she tied them for the five hundredth time while Andy and I circled the parking lot and my family disappeared down the sidewalk, she tried to stand up. She looked like a newborn calf or deer with her spindly legs that kept buckling under her.

"Gene, can you help Lark?" Corinne asked. She skated away with Andy, not waiting for an answer.

"Hey!" I yelled after them. Lark, who was about to wipe out again, grabbed onto me.

"Thank you, Gene," Lark said. She was an inch or so taller than me so it was a good thing I had decent balance and strength. It was kind of like having a giraffe as your Siamese twin. "I don't know what I'd do without you," Lark said solemnly. She got her balance enough to let go of my coat but then put her hand in mine.

I know what I'd do without you, I thought, watching Andy and Corinne skate down the sidewalk. *I'd skate Andy into the ground. Then I'd take on Corinne.* "We'd better go or we'll lose them." I grabbed both her hands and pulled her as I skated backwards. I weaved in and out of the handful of people on the sidewalk. Corinne and Andy had set this up. Andy probably thought it was hilarious.

"I can't keep up," Lark complained. I sighed and slowed down. It wasn't her fault she was ruining my life. "Not a very big turnout," she said, as we reached the Cathedral where the march was supposed to start.

"Yeah." I glanced at the straggly group gathering on the Cathedral lawn. "Maybe people feel too depressed to come."

"Did you know him?" she asked in this intense way that made me want to skate away from her as fast as I could.

"Who?" I said, even though I knew who she was talking about.

"What was he like?" She looked in my face with her big mascara-fringed eyes.

"Who, Wellstone?" I asked, just to point out that in the U.S. we don't necessarily have to continue the same deadly conversation all day long. "He was nice." I realized how lame I sounded. "He made you feel like he wanted to know you," I added, remembering how he talked to me about sports and stuff.

I thought about his book, and how I'd never bothered to finish it. All of a sudden, I felt really bad I hardly read it at all. Really really bad. I felt Lark looking at me. I skated a little faster.

"Oh, my God!" she said as we turned the corner to the other side of the Cathedral. The hill was a mass of people, thousands of them, all bundled up against the cold, singing "Give Peace a Chance," carrying peace signs and Wellstone lawn signs. I squinted to read what people had written on the Wellstone signs: CARRY IT FORWARD. Mom would like that, I thought. I could just imagine her pointing it out to Dad.

"Do you see Andy and Corinne?" I asked.

"My God, how will we ever find them?" Lark sounded fake like she was glad to have me in her manicured European clutches.

I considered ditching her, but I noticed she was holding my hand really tight and giving me this uncertain smile. Then I felt bad for her. It must have been weird being in a foreign country all by yourself even if you were sophisticated and had mastered the parental discussion. Especially if you got stuck in a situation where you were inline skating for the first time with someone who was not old before their time, someone who had absolutely no interest in you and what came out of your lip-glossed mouth.

"Have you ever been to one of these before?" Lark asked.

"Yeah. My parents are so into peace marches and demonstrations I probably took my first steps at one of these."

Lark laughed. She had a nice laugh. There was something about her laugh, her voice—a little syrupy but it warmed you up and had a little kick. Kind of like drinking a mocha latte.

"You're so lucky to have such great parents. My mother and father are very strict. They'd be afraid to let me go, like I'd be corrupted or in danger or something."

"Really? How did you get them to let you come to the U.S.?"

Lark laughed again. "They think Minnesota is all wholesome farm country. Besides it is a great academic honor to be an exchange student. How could they possibly let me pass up this opportunity?"

"So do you, like, lie to them?" I asked.

"Not really lie," she said as the crowd closed around us and started moving. "Just rearrange the truth, you know. I'll tell them about coming to this with your parents and Lily, but I probably won't mention that we took the detour to the contest."

"The contest?" Maybe I'd underestimated her.

I stopped in my tracks, realizing we were probably heading in the wrong direction. This was a big mistake as some crabby ladies carrying signs that said NURSES FOR PEACE bashed into me. "You shouldn't be in those without a helmet." One of them pointed down at my skates.

"Thank you for reminding us," Lark said. "We must retrieve them." She tugged on me to leave the march and go down a side street.

"Do you know where to go?" I asked.

"Don't you?"

"Andy just told me about it in the car." Just because it was my country and I was a guy, I shouldn't have been expected to know everything.

"Corinne said it was at the red umbrella building on Fifth Street right before Rice Park. You know where Rice Park is right?"

"Yeah, I guess so."

"Come on." She yanked my arm. "I think I see Corinne and Andy ahead."

I followed her, noticing she was getting more steady on her feet. I didn't see Corinne or Andy anywhere and I wondered if Lark knew what she was talking about. As we skated away from the crowd, I noticed we were heading straight down. Downtown. It would have been a great skate if I'd been with a good skater.

Just when I was getting nervous there was no way we'd find this place, Lark said, "There they are!" She let go of my hand and almost wiped out. I looked for Andy's fire-hydrant-red stocking cap and actually saw it bobbing in a group of people huddled together. Above them was a tower that said Travelers in big black letters next to a red umbrella. Travelers Insurance.

We skated up to them and I could kind of see they were watching somebody skate down a rail into a big concrete plaza.

Corinne turned to us. "We could do better," she said to me, a little too loud. Some guys turned and looked at me, like it was my fault she didn't know when to shut up.

"I didn't see it," I muttered.

"That guy was good, "Andy said, oblivious to the rest of us. This at least convinced the thugs to turn back to the competition.

I craned my neck and watched the next guy fly down the rail backwards.

"Wow, do you do this?" Lark asked me, her voice melting my insides to molten latte again.

"Hey, I do it too," Corinne butted in.

"Why don't you just shut up since you're not doing it now," one of the thugs said to her.

"You think I can't skate better than any of these assholes?" Corinne said.

The group started leaving. We'd just caught the end of it, which sucked.

"My turn," said Corinne as everyone turned away.

"Wait," the one thug guy said to his friends. "I've got to watch big-mouth fall flat on her face." He turned to Corinne. "The party's over. Didn't you know girls weren't invited?"

"How old are these gays?" Lark said to Corinne. "They act like small boys on the playground."

"Hey, did you just call us gay?" The thug's toady friend asked.

"She's French," the other guy said. "*Voulez-vous coucher avec moi?*" He smirked.

Lark blasted him with a string of Dutch I was sure her parents wouldn't approve of. This was so entertaining we almost missed the main show, but then of course Corinne, that hotdog, wouldn't let us do that. "Hey, losers check this out," she yelled.

Everyone turned as she skipped the rail and instead cleared the stairs backwards. Then she skated over to these big granite planters and jumped from one level to the next grinding them. She kept going, finding everything in this stone wonderland to dance on. The thugs' mouths were gaping.

Andy said, "That's my bionic babe." Something I found pathetic maybe because I wished I could say it.

"That's one sexy chick," Lark said. The thugs didn't disagree.

"You wanna try, Gene?" Corinne skated up to me.

"No way," I said. I just wanted to watch her.

"How about one of you?" she said to the goons.

"No skates." One of them shrugged.

"We gotta go," said the other one.

"Oops." Andy looked at his watch. "So do we."

We headed toward the Capitol. The girls were in front talking to each other nonstop, so fast I wondered if Corinne spoke Dutch. Andy and I didn't say much. I wondered if he felt the same way I did. Like I was still up there with Corinne flying through the air.

"So what do you think of her?" Andy asked.

"She's incredible," I said. If I didn't start working my butt off, I'd never catch up with her.

"Yeah, when Corinne said she liked you, I said we should get the two of you together."

"Really?" A blast of wind almost blew me past Andy and I had to work to slow myself down. So Corinne liked me and it really was Andy's idea to get us together yesterday? "Wow, thanks," I said. He was a better friend than I could have ever imagined.

"Well, she is kind of cute in her blonde European Barbie way."

"Lark?" The wind was so strong I almost ran into him.

"Well, yeah, who'd you think I was talking about?"

"I'm just surprised to hear you think Lark's cute. She doesn't seem like your type," I tried to cover.

"She's not. She's *your* type," he told me.

Chapter Eleven

Angels and Martyrs

On Monday morning, Mr. Mac stood in front of the class, not saying anything. This was so creepy everyone stopped talking once the final bell rang and just sat there. Finally, he took a deep breath, exhaled and said, "Instead of talking about our political system today, I think it's important to take some time to talk about one of our politicians." He turned and wrote PAUL WELLSTONE in big block letters at the top of the whiteboard, pressing the marker so hard it squeaked.

"Give me a break," Derrick Martin complained. "This school is so liberal it makes me sick. I don't have to listen to this left wing indoctrination." He got up to leave.

"Sit down, Mr. Martin," Mr. Mac said in this soft, but scary, voice that made Derrick shut up and drop to his seat like a deflated balloon.

"Paul Wellstone," Mr. Mac paced back and forth like he was wound up so tight he'd never relax again, "was not a typical politician. He was not a typical Democrat. He was not a typical U.S. senator. He was unique, not because of his political views, but because of his view of politics."

Everyone gaped at him, their faces forming a collective "huh?" I didn't know where he was going with this, but I did know he was right. Paul Wellstone was different and I wanted Mr. Mac to explain why.

"Paul Wellstone was a grassroots community organizer," Mr. Mac continued. He stopped abruptly in front of Tiffany Peterson, who stood out from the rest of the class in a puffy pink sweater, the color of Pepto-Bismol. "Ms. Peterson," he asked, "can you tell us what that means?"

"He was an organized farmer?" Tiffany Peterson, who had this stunted idea that acting dumb made her attractive, shrugged and smiled.

"Ahh, yes, Wellstone did organize farmers." Mr. Mac was on the move again, not letting Tiffany's dumb act slow him down. "He got people together who didn't have power—family farmers, the families of the mentally ill, poor people. He organized them, and when they joined together, they were able to change government policy. Paul Wellstone saw that power came from the people who put him in power—not from cutting deals with the insiders."

"But . . ." Derrick Martin may have sat down, but he was having a hard time keeping quiet.

Mr. Mac raced over to Derrick's desk and interrupted him. "It made him sick to see Democrats more concerned about raising money and winning elections than serving their constituents. He was concerned about values. About standing up for people and doing what was right. That's why so many people who disagreed with him on the issues voted for him anyway." Mr. Mac shook his wild head of hair up and down to make his point. "Even Republicans, Mr. Martin, even Republicans."

"People, I want you to remember this." Mr. Mac headed toward his desk. "Paul Wellstone did not feel politics was a bad word. This is what he said." He grabbed a book from his desk. It was Paul Wellstone's book, a copy of the one I had barely started. He thumbed through it, found his place and read, "Politics is not

98

about money or power games, or winning for the sake of winning. Politics is about the improvement of people's lives." He put the book down. "The improvement of people's lives," he repeated.

"He did not want *you* . . ." He slammed his fist on the desk and we all jumped. "To be cynical. He wanted young people to be engaged in the important issues of our time."

It's true I thought, as the bell rang and Mr. Mac collapsed in his chair. Paul Wellstone did want my opinion on Iraq. He wasn't just being nice to a kid. My eyes started watering, and I had to force myself to stop hearing him say, "I want your vote, Gene." I felt Lark looking at me as everybody left. It was like she knew this secret about me. Even though I didn't tell her. I knew Paul Wellstone and somehow knowing him changed me.

"Mr. Mac was mental today." I heard Derrick say as we crowded out the door. I stopped and stepped back inside because I didn't want to be around Derrick Martin or anyone right then. Mr. Mac was standing at the board, scrubbing it with the eraser. But Paul Wellstone's name wouldn't come off. He'd accidentally written it in permanent marker.

The rest of my day at school was miserable. I felt wrung out, like I'd been crying even though I hadn't let myself cry at all. It was almost a relief that Andy was ignoring me and was totally focused on Corinne. Then there was Lark, who seemed to be lurking around our shared locker whenever I needed to get something. At least I had my nonexistent love life to distract me.

What did Andy have that I didn't have, I asked myself as I collapsed on the couch after school. I ate an entire bag of potato chips while Yellow stared up at me. Just good looks, bizarre creative genius, a totally weird secondhand wardrobe . . . Corinne—that was all. I'd never had a girlfriend and Andy was on his third one, fourth if you counted grade school. "You and I have a lot in common," I told Yellow, tossed him a chip and watched him dive for it. "We're both pathetic."

I thought back to Corinne's skating on Saturday. I wondered if I could have skated that well if I'd gotten my good skates back. I wondered if Corinne would ever watch me skate and feel like I did when I watched her: like this rush of adrenaline and desire was racing through my body. Dre Powell. I had to get a Dre Powell DVD and work on skating like him. That was when I decided to see Sister Jude and offer to finish whatever she thought was left on the fence to get my skates back. They were the only thing I had that Andy didn't. Skating was the only thing that was mine. Corinne's and mine.

It was deserted at the Stairs. No nuns or homeless people in sight. I went to the side door and walked the unlit hall to Sister Jude's office. Her door was open but there was no light coming from it. I peered in anyway, and there was Sister Jude hunched over her desk writing away. "You should have a light on. You'll hurt your eyes," I said, realizing I sounded like my mom.

"The light hurts my eyes." Sister Jude looked up from her papers. "Sit down, Eugene. I need to talk to you."

I sat down, and she kept working like I wasn't there. I looked around, trying to estimate the ratio of angels to martyrs on her shelves and walls. I squinted at a painting of a guy. St. Stephen, it said on a plastic label on the frame. He had blood dripping from arrows stuck all over his body. Cool but creepy. I wondered if anyone else other than maybe some guy at Marvel comics had such bizarre stuff on their walls. I went completely around the room trying to count. There was a lot of stuff everywhere. I had finally figured out that it was more or less tied: angels = martyrs, when she looked up from her desk surprised to still see me there.

"Eugene," she said, "I just wanted to finish this one section of our budget. I guess I'm a little distracted these days."

"That's okay." I realized as my eyes adjusted to the dim light, that she'd been crying. I sighed. I couldn't stand being around all of these people who used to have it together and were falling apart. I wondered if Paul Wellstone had any idea how much everyone depended on him to make sure everything turned out all right. I wondered why his stupid plane had to crash anyway.

"You probably came for your skates."

"Well, yeah."

She took the picture of her with Paul Wellstone and the vets down from the shelf and looked at it with a faraway look that reminded me of how my mom looked at pictures of me and Lily when we were little. She put it in front of me. I realized that one of the vets, he was younger and heavier there, was Billy.

"Did you ever hear the story about Wellstone's big mistake?" she asked.

"Mistake?" As far as I knew, everybody acted like he was this perfect person whose only mistake was to get on that airplane.

"When he was first elected. He wanted to make a statement against the Iraq War."

"They've been talking about it for that long?"

"Different Iraq War, honey. Desert Storm. Bush's father's war," she explained.

"Wow." I guess there were too many wars for me to keep track of.

"Anyway, he gave this big arrogant speech in front of the Vietnam Memorial. Offended everyone."

"Paul Wellstone?"

"Yes, honey. Then do you know what he did after everyone made fun of him and his political career was going down the toilet?"

"Ran away?" That's what I would have done.

She sighed like my answer made her even sadder. "He apologized." Her eyes brightened like she was remembering something happy. "Not only that, but he became a voice for vets—the people he pissed off the most. He helped people like Billy because of his mistake." She looked down at the picture. "Billy loved Paul Wellstone," she said. "Did you know Paul had a brother who was mentally ill?"

"No." I wondered why she was telling me all this.

"I hate apologizing."

I shrugged. Of course she hated apologizing. She hated admitting she was wrong. It was like she expected everyone to pretend she was perfect or something just because she was a nun.

"I'm sorry, Eugene." She looked uncomfortable. "I thought it was a good idea having one of the kids who wrecked Billy's camp work with him. To get to know him as a person. To stop thinking of him as a freak."

"I don't think of Billy as a freak." She was doing it again, assuming the worst about me. "Could I have my skates now?"

"That's what I'm trying to tell you, honey." She looked like a shrunken, uncertain version of herself. "Your skates are gone, and Billy's gone too. I think he took them."

"He took them?"

She fumbled around in her desk drawer, pulled out some crumpled bills and handed them to me. "I'm sorry that's all I've got—but I want you to have something. You did good work."

"No thanks." I tried to hand the money back. It was just a few dollars, nothing that would help replace a pair of $300 skates. Besides, I couldn't take food out of the mouths of homeless people or cigarettes away from Sister Jude. "I need my skates," I told her.

"Keep it," she ordered, turning back into the Sister Jude I was used to.

I kept the money wadded in my fist. "I need my skates," I repeated. "Why would Billy take my skates?"

"I don't know. I'm not sure why Billy does anything."

"I didn't do anything to him."

"He's going through one of his bad periods. And I was distracted by everything and didn't notice he'd stopped taking his medication." She looked like she might cry again.

"My skates," I said. "I need my skates." Then I got really pathetic. "I love my skates."

"I know that, honey," Sister Jude said. "I think Billy knew that too. Maybe that's why he took them."

"That doesn't make sense."

"He didn't used to be like this." She blinked at me like all of the sudden she'd figured out how to once again make me useful. "You know, honey, he may try to reach you, or maybe he expects you to find him. You need to let me know if you hear from him. I need to get his medicine to him. I need to know he's okay."

"Yeah," I said, because I didn't know what else to tell her. I almost wished we had blown him up that night with the fireworks. All he'd done since then was to try to ruin my life. Then I felt guilty because for some reason Sister Jude cared what happened to him. But I figured that was her job.

I stood up. "Well, I gotta go."

"You'll let me know if you hear from him? It's important, Eugene, very important." She wouldn't let this go, which annoyed me because it seemed like she cared more about that old bum Billy than about me and my skates.

"Yeah," I said. And she turned back to her work, ignoring me again.

While she wasn't looking, I took the wad of money and dropped it on her desk. The picture of the vets and Paul Wellstone looked back at me. I'd missed that one in my count. Was he an angel or a martyr, I wondered. Martyr, I decided. The martyrs won.

The Wellstone Memorial service was scheduled on the same night as Dad's birthday. "You're not going, are you?" I asked at supper a few days before, thinking how I didn't want to miss his birthday dinner and cake.

"Of course I'm going," Dad said. "We're all going. It's what I want for my birthday."

"Can't we just watch it on TV?"

"Gene, I invited your friend to go with us," Mom said.

"What friend?" I asked, wondering what friend of mine would accept an invitation to go with my weird family to a memorial service.

"Lark."

Chapter Twelve

Memorial

The doorbell rang.

"Gene, get the door," Mom ordered, walking out of the room with Lily tagging along behind her.

"Why can't you get it?" I complained, not moving from the couch.

"The timer just rang for Dad's cake," Mom said from the kitchen. Even though we were going to the memorial service that night at least she was baking a cake for Dad's birthday.

"Lily can get it." I didn't move. Maybe if I stalled long enough the person who we knew was waiting would give up.

"Gene!"

I groaned, dragged myself to the door, then opened it.

Lark stood there dressed completely in black. She was wearing tight black jeans, a black T-shirt, black boots. The only thing that wasn't black was her bright red lipstick. She smiled at me like she knew she looked good.

I didn't smile back.

"Gotta get my skates," I muttered, disappearing up the stairs, leaving her standing there.

If I skated to the memorial service, I could escape my family and Lark who were planning to walk there. Then I could look for Billy. I knew he'd be there. He was so into being one of Paul Wellstone's vets. I'd skate him down and get my Shimas back. I had to get my skates back.

When I clomped down the stairs in my skates, my whole family was standing there looking disgusted with me. Lark looked embarrassed.

"You're not wearing those to the service," Mom said.

"I've got my shoes in my pack."

She just shook her head, not saying anything because what she really wanted to do was lecture me about being nice to my imaginary friend Lark.

"Happy Birthday," Lark said to Dad as we headed out. I ended up behind her and her tight jeans. She really did look good. "I brought you this small gift."

"Thanks." Dad took this fancy little wrapped box from her and raised his eyebrows like he was worried it was jewelry.

"Open it! Open it!" Lily demanded.

"We have to get going," Dad said.

"Take it with you," Lark suggested. "You won't regret it."

We walked out the door as Dad opened the present and Lily said, "Chocolate!"

"Belgian chocolate," Lark said. "The best chocolate in the world."

I snorted.

"Belgian chocolate is the best chocolate in the world," Dad, the know-it-all, informed me. "Thank you, Lark. I don't have to share, do I?"

"You'd better," Mom said. "Or we'll steal it."

He passed around the box and we each took one. We'd almost made it to the river and I hadn't skated ahead yet. "What do you think, Gene?" Dad asked, as the most intense best chocolate I'd ever had in my life melted in my mouth. Lark looked at me like my answer would determine the entire future of our nonexistent relationship.

"Almost as good as a Kit Kat bar."

"What?" Dad had a fit. "Why did I waste the best choco-late in the world on him?" He threw up his arms in fake agony.

"Gene's lying," Lily said. "This is really, really good," she told Lark. "Look. He's smiling."

I tried not to smile, but it was pretty darn good. I noticed we'd reached the river and there I was still hanging out with Lark and my family. I looked over at her. She was smiling her red-lipped smile. She was sneaky, that Lark.

"This makes up for leaving the cake," Mom said. I could tell she was feeling guilty about Dad not having much of a birthday celebration. She didn't have to worry. This would be one birthday we'd always remember. The river was uncoiling next to us like a big lazy snake. It felt like we were on an adven-ture, not going to a funeral.

"M-I-S-S-I-S-S-I-P-P-I," Lily spelled.

"Wait until I tell my parents I walked tonight by the Mississippi River," Lark said. For her we lived in this magic place with a famous river down the road.

Mom took a deep breath. "I love the smell along the river this time of year. It smells like fall, like a big pile of leaves."

"It smells like chocolate," Lily said. "Is there any left?"

"Later, Lil," Dad told her. "You're supposed to savor it."

We were all quiet as we savored the big muddy slug of water unwinding by our side and the crunch of leaves as we walked through them. We headed up toward the U to the memorial service. It was in Williams Arena where the Gophers basketball team usually played. I skated ahead but had to turn back. There were people everywhere. I realized I could lose my family in a second.

"Wow," Lark said, reminding me of when she saw the crowd at the peace rally. She must have thought all we did was gather in crowds. Which was all we did at that point.

We got in a line that went around the block, but moved pretty fast into the building. I scrambled to exchange my skates for the shoes in my pack. Nobody checked my pack. They just handed me a program and a Wellstone green button that had one of his slogans on it: "Stand up / Keep Fighting."

"Security's not very tight." Dad glanced at my backpack.

"I think they have other things on their minds," Mom said.

I'd just noticed a group of guys there who had signs that said they were vets. I checked them out but they seemed to have better personal hygiene than Billy. If he was there, he was probably lurking in the shadows. Thousands of people filed into the auditorium. Looking for Billy was like looking at a page of *Where's Waldo*.

We had good seats in the volunteer section, thanks to my parents. Mom and Lily sat on either side of Lark. Lark gave me this look, like I was supposed to butt in and do something about it. I just shrugged and sat at the end of the row next to my dad.

"Who is that man?" Lark pointed to this black guy in a suit walking around the main floor shaking hands with everybody and dazzling them with his smile. "Is he a movie star?"

"No, he just thinks he is," Dad said. "That's Jesse Jackson."

"When he ran for president, Paul ran his Minnesota campaign. The Rainbow Coalition," Mom explained.

"Oh, I've heard of him," Lark said. "He, how do you say it, oozes with the charisma." Just then Jesse Jackson looked up in our direction, grinned and waved. "Oooh," Lark said and all the females around us, including Lily, started sighing over this guy like they just couldn't help themselves.

"Oozes is about right," Dad said snidely to me. In anticipation of Dad's entertaining play by play, I congratulated myself on getting the best seat assignment.

By the time the service started, I'd given up looking for Billy. It was just too big of a crowd and I didn't see a lot of Billy types. Most of the people there seemed to have taken a bath lately. They showed all these famous people making their entrances on big screens hanging over the stage. When Bill Clinton, yeah, the Bill Clinton who used to be president, came on screen smiling down on everyone, Dad laughed and said really loud to me over the noise of the crowd, "I can't believe they're playing "Love Train"—now that guy really oozes with the charisma." When the couple of Republicans who dared to come showed up on the screen everybody booed. Everybody but us. Dad started to boo, but Mom elbowed him and leaned over to glare at me. I knew she was right but she wasn't very fun.

There was all this music which was really good, especially the gospel stuff. This folk singer, Ann Reed sang this song about heroes, which made Dad get tears in his eyes. It was weird, I'd never thought of my dad having a hero. I thought that when you were an adult you were supposed to be one.

Each person who died in the plane crash had someone who talked about them. My favorite was the brother of this guy Will, who drove Paul Wellstone's car. He told a story about how Will's car had tinted windows so no one could see in. How Paul Wellstone would jump up and down and wave, trying to get the attention of anybody in traffic who had a Wellstone bumper sticker, and he couldn't understand why everyone ignored him. Will, of course, was having too good of a time watching him make a fool of himself to tell him. This cracked me up but it also made me feel sad all of the sudden. I guess deep down I wanted to be one of those guys who worked for Paul Wellstone. How could I have missed him so much when I hardly knew him? It was like I missed taking for granted that he'd be there for me. That he'd be in my future.

I finally had to get up to go to the bathroom. I couldn't believe how long this thing was lasting. Lark, who had probably been watching my every move, followed me. "I need to freshen up," she said, like she was some ancient rich lady. I noticed her lips were kind of faded.

"I need to take a piss," I said, just to point out I was fifteen not eighty.

"That too." She laughed her laugh that I couldn't help but like and I had to give her credit for not saying she had to go tinkle or urinate.

We found the bathrooms and Lark said, "Gene, will you wait for me? It's so intimidating here. I'm afraid I'll get lost."

"Sure." What else could I say? At least she couldn't follow me into the men's room. After I peed, I looked at myself in the mirror. What did Lark see in me anyway? I guessed I was good-looking in an ordinary way. I wasn't a zit face and even though my hair wasn't as cool as Brady's, it was basically cool. I mean it wasn't a mullet or anything. My mom always said I had soulful eyes. I guess because they're brown. Soulful. Sounded like something European girls would like. I smiled into the mirror, your generic TV commercial post-orthodontia smile. Just then, some guy walked in and gave me a weird look. "Got something stuck in my teeth," I muttered on the way out. Why did these girls make me do these stupid things? Girls.

"It sounds very intense in there." Lark finally came out and gestured toward the stadium.

"Yeah," I agreed, noticing how I couldn't help but feel my insides melt a bit as she smiled her red smile. "I guess we'd better get back in."

"I guess," she echoed. She reached over and pushed my hair back. "It was in your eyes," she explained.

We found our way back to our seats as they introduced this guy Rick who as supposed to be Paul Wellstone's best friend. It was weird because he didn't tell sad, funny stories like everybody else. He started yelling about how we had to win this election for Paul Wellstone. Everybody was on their feet, yelling and clapping. He asked everybody, even Republicans, to help win this election for Paul Wellstone.

I got the creeps because what he was saying felt so familiar and then I remembered. It was just me and Paul Wellstone at the state fair and he was giving me that intense eager dog look and telling me, "Gene, I want your vote." I finally got it. I had to do everything I could to help him win, to help his cause win, even if I couldn't vote. Maybe that would make up for blowing off him and his book, for blowing off school on the day he died.

I'd never seen this place go so berserk. Even when the Gophers were winning. Dad was yelling. So I stood next to him and yelled too. It felt like everybody, everybody in the whole place was yelling, yelling the sadness out of their bodies. There were tears streaming down Dad's face but it finally seemed okay. It felt like everybody was turning all this sadness into something so strong it felt good, like hope, I guess. Like maybe everything was going to be okay after all.

When we left it was like this big river of people pouring out into the streets. I wanted to say to Lark and Lily, "It's a human Mississippi." But it was too loud and crowded for conversation, and I could barely hear my mom ask my dad in this confused voice, "What just happened?" Dad just shook his head. Whatever happened, I was glad. People were talking and pushing into each other. It was so much better than that dead peace parade.

I saw someone up ahead in an old army jacket with a straggly ponytail. I sped up and got close enough to grab his arm. Some guy I'd never seen before turned to me and said, "Gotta a problem?"

"Uh, sorry," I said. "I thought you were somebody else."

I turned to find my family but they were swallowed by the crowd. Then I saw Lark looking freaked out. "Gene!" She grabbed my arm. "I tried to follow you but then I lost everyone." I slowed down so we were side by side but she didn't let go. She hung on to my arm, which wasn't so bad since she really did look good.

We headed down the street, then down to the river, away from the crowd. The river snaked past us, and the light from the street lamps made Lark look mysterious and European in her black clothes. "Wow, I feel depleted," she said, finally letting go of me.

"Yeah," I agreed, even though that wasn't exactly the word I would've used. I felt wiped out and buzzed all at the same time.

"Do you think he would have liked it?" Lark asked.

"Paul Wellstone? Yeah, he would have loved it." I felt good to be certain about this and that I was there. "It was like him," I tried to explain. "All enthusiastic and emotional and about important things without being boring."

"Good," she said. "I am glad for him."

"Yeah," I agreed. In her weird European way, Lark explained why I felt better.

She plopped down on a bench. "Skate for me?"

"Skate?"

"Yeah." She stretched out on the bench like a cat and smiled at me.

"These are my old skates." I put them on. "They kind of limit me."

"You move . . . well . . . I like the way you move." She covered her face and started to giggle, which made me feel both embarrassed at what she'd said and relieved she was capable of being a goofy teenage girl.

I considered the way I felt when I watched Corinne. The difference was I'd never have the nerve to tell her. "Okay." I started skating backwards, knowing that even something that easy looked good to someone who knew nothing. I skated forward really fast and did a basic 360.

"Wow!" Lark said. "How do you do that? Aren't you afraid of falling?" The street lamp lit up her yellow hair as she flung it back and tilted her head toward me.

"Not really." I skated away fast again, then tripped on purpose when I got closer.

"Oh, my God." She ran up to me. I faked having a hard time getting up. Then popped up as she tried to help me.

"See, I can fall down and get up anytime I want. Good trick, huh?"

She pretended to be mad at me, but ended up laughing her Belgian chocolate laugh. "Don't you get hurt doing things like that?"

"Sure." I pulled up my pant leg. "Want to see some of my scars?"

She bent close to me. I don't know how this happened. I really don't—but all of a sudden I was kissing her.

So, this hot European girl in black, who you must admit you find attractive, okay very attractive, but if you have to be honest does kind of bug you, throws herself at you. What do you do?

A. Think, well at least I can be friends with Andy and Corinne again. At least now my life will be less complicated.
B. Think, the things I do for Andy and Corinne. The sacrifices I make. I am such a martyr.
C. Think, this really isn't my fault. Andy and Corinne, my mom, even my little sister pushed this girl at me.
D. Stop thinking, you idiot.

CHAPTER THIRTEEN

MIDNIGHT MADNESS

How could I have ever thought my life would be less complicated? The next morning, before school, there was no escaping Lark. She turned up at our locker, nonstop touching me, and I kept wondering if everybody was looking at us because they thought we looked good together or because they noticed she was about an inch taller than me without my skates.

At least Corinne seemed kind of jealous, which was enjoyable. Andy and the rest of my friends were in awe of me. Like I'd gone to this foreign country and came back another person. Brady acted embarrassed he still had to share a locker with Lark and me. "Could you like take your public displays of affection like somewhere else?" he asked.

"Could you take your sweatshirt out of our locker for a moment?" Lark asked him as she untangled herself from me and dug in her purse. "Thanks," she said, wrinkling her nose, as she sprayed his sweatshirt with some kind of perfume. "Now it won't stink up my stuff."

"Aww, man," Brady complained. "Can't you do something about her?"

I shrugged. *No, I couldn't. I couldn't do anything about her at all.*

It wasn't just Lark. Everything that had seemed great about that memorial service was all wrong. Each morning, my dad pointed this out.

114

"More weird letters about the memorial service," Dad said at breakfast on Friday. "I can't believe it's still getting all this attention." He drank his coffee, then turned back to the paper. "Listen to this," he said. "If Wellstone's legacy is the political circus that was his memorial service, let's elect Coleman."

Lily looked up from the comics, which she had stolen from me as usual. "I didn't see any circus."

"It's just a way of criticizing it, Lil," Dad explained.

"I don't get it," said Mom. "What does one person crazy with grief have to do with the election?"

"It was a whole field house crazy with grief."

"That's mean," Lily protested. "That mem-or-i-al (she said this like she was reading it from the dictionary) service was comfortable."

"Huh?" I said.

"Do you mean comforting, Lily?" Mom, the interpreter of dweebs, asked.

"Well," said Lily. "We were miserable when Paul Wellstone died. That memorial service made us comfortable again."

Our family sat around the table considering this. My parents and I nodded our heads. "Comfortable," Dad agreed.

Finally, it was the night before the election and we were on our way to this Midnight Madness thing to distribute leaflets for Walter Mondale. He was this old guy who used to be vice president of the United States who was running in place of Wellstone. We got extra credit for Mr. Mac's class. And, as Andy said, extra credit from our parents.

"My parents are getting progressively weirder about this whole election," he complained. "They even put up a lawn sign I made as a joke that x'd out Coleman. I said, 'don't you think it's offensive' and they said 'so what—Coleman's alive—

what's he got to complain about?' We've got to win this just to get them back to normal."

"Yeah," I agreed. "It's like this whole Wellstone thing has made all of them even weirder than usual."

My mom drove that night. We picked up the girls after Andy came over to our house. They came out of Corinne's in their skates. Lark was wearing a pair of shiny tight pants that looked like they were made out of leather and a red turtleneck. Corinne had on low-rider jeans that were strategically aerated and a Bob Marley T-shirt that would have been too small on Lily. I wondered how two girls could look so different and both look so good. Andy and I looked pretty basic even though I'd spent twenty minutes (according to Lily) trying to get my hair right.

"I hope there's a good turnout," Mom worried as we headed toward Lake Street.

"Don't worry, Mom," I said. "There's five of us. We can get a lot done."

"Especially in our skates," Andy added.

"Where are your good skates, Gene?" Mom glanced down at my feet. "You never wear them anymore."

"I need new parts for them, remember?" I got this nervous feeling in my stomach. I had to get them back before she and my dad found out what had happened. I wasn't sure how I'd gotten away with lying to my parents about this, especially with Sister Jude involved. She'd been working on my mom to volunteer at her soup kitchen.

"What's going on here?' Mom asked as we reached Lake Street and all of the sudden there were people and cars everywhere. There was this incredible line snaking out of the Carpenters Union.

"I think they got a good turnout, Mrs. Snow," Andy said.

"All of South Minneapolis," Lark agreed.

"Maybe they don't need us after all," Andy said. "We could go to Taco Bell instead. I'm hungry."

We all gave him a hard time. My mom, of course, saw us as the most important people there. Lark and Corinne wanted to be part of the scene, which did look like a lot of fun. I just wanted to be part of it, part of winning.

We had to park blocks away and skate in slow motion not to leave Mom behind as we headed toward the line. It was like this giant party. Everyone was laughing and talking even though it was probably past some of these old peoples' bedtimes. We finally got up by the door where there was some official guy joking about how he should get some kids to pull up Coleman lawn signs. Mom wanted to get out of line to lecture him.

"I can't believe he'd even joke about something like that," she complained. Andy and I looked at each other over her head. We'd been planning to go over to Derrick Martin's and trash his Coleman sign. It figured we'd get the official kindergarten disapproval.

By the time we got in the building, practically everyone else had picked up their leaflets and moved outside to listen to some speeches. We went to get our assignment and found out that the only thing left was this industrial wasteland over by the University. Mom was frowning. I knew she felt responsible for insuring that we had a safe boring time. She probably thought we'd do our own neighborhood. That would have been a big fat waste of time since most of our neighborhood was there.

"Hey, you kids can't have skates on in here!" Some lady marched up to us.

I could feel Corinne tensing up next to me, getting ready to verbally let her have it. I leaned over and started pulling my skates off because I perversely knew that the smell of my socks would make that lady and Corinne shut up. Just then this old guy came in and walked right up to us. He walked past the enforcement lady who tried to get his attention, and Mom and all of the other adults standing around. He shook my hand, then Corinne and Lark's. Then he fake punched Andy on the shoulder.

"Look at this great group of volunteers. I bet you cover a lot of ground in those." He pointed down at Andy's skates and punched him again. Andy started to give him his quizzical eyebrow look, where his eyebrows looked like two caterpillars on the move, when my mom got his attention, mouthing Mondale. Lark clapped her hands together and squealed.

"Manhole?" Andy said, his caterpillars arching their backs. "Oh." He gave his big goofy smile as he finally got it. "Yes, sir, a lot of ground."

"Keep it up," Walter Mondale urged. "You're the best volunteers I have." He walked past us and out the door. You could hear the crowd outside clapping and yelling.

One thing about meeting Walter Mondale was it made us all totally committed to leafleting. Corinne, who just couldn't keep her mouth shut, sweetly asked the lady with the rules if maybe she wanted us to leave and go work for the Republicans.

"He kind of reminds me of Dumbledore in *Harry Potter*," Andy said, rubbing his shoulder. "He hits pretty hard for an old guy."

We took off once we convinced my mom that going to this bombed-out part of town would complete our educational experience. I figured it was another chance for me to look for Billy. I skated to the river every day looking for him, but the most that ever happened was I got the creeps wondering if somebody was watching me. I had to find other bum hangouts.

My mom let me drive up and down the winding streets in Prospect Park, this neighborhood that bordered where we were heading. We went by the Witch's Tower, this spooky old water tower that looked like a witch's hat.

Mom kept telling me to slow down. It was so embarrassing that I sped up a little. The streets were pretty narrow and I almost swiped a couple of parked cars. "Snowman," Andy said from behind me. "Your driving is so sketchy."

"It's making me apprehensive," Lark agreed.

"It sucks," added Corinne.

"Shut up." I turned around to glare at them and Mom had to grab the steering wheel.

"Eugene Snow, if you don't start to pay attention and drive like a reasonable person, your driving practice is going to be over for tonight and for the foreseeable future," Mom lectured.

I stared straight ahead and slowed down to what I imagined was the pace of an elderly librarian driving a model T, my mother's idea of a reasonable person.

"There's many cars here," Lark pointed out. "Shouldn't we be pamphleting them?"

"Leafleting," I corrected under my breath. I was trying not to be so critical of the way Lark talked. It was hard when everyone was so critical of the way I drove.

"This isn't our area yet," Mom said. "Turn left up here, Gene."

I turned left. Away from the winding hilly streets crowded with cars onto a deserted street that was perfectly flat and straight, bordered by factories and empty lots instead of cool old houses. "This is it," Mom announced.

"Eew," Lark said.

"What are we supposed to do here?" Andy asked. "Get out the ghost vote?"

Mom sighed as I parked in front of this old warehouse. It looked like the kind of place where bums might camp out. I didn't know how I was ever going to find Billy.

"Wait. Look," Lark said. Her perfume hit me as she leaned up from the back seat and pointed past my face to the front window.

"Mmm," I said, inhaling instead of looking. She jabbed my shoulder and I peered ahead.

"Look at all those cars!" Corinne described what I thought I was seeing: an enormous surface lot packed with cars.

"It must take up a whole block," Andy said.

"Let's go for it." I revved the engine.

"That's it, Gene," Mom said. "Move over. I'm driving."

"I was in park, Mom. It's not like you can crash into anybody in park."

"If anyone could, you could," said Andy, who, as far as I could figure, was jealous because he had never driven anyone anywhere.

My mom drove us the pathetic block and a half. I didn't even feel like getting out of the car. It was midnight and I was mad. Midnight madness.

"Let's race." Corinne pulled Andy out of the car. "Us two against you guys." She grabbed a pile of leaflets and they took off. I put on my skates and turned to Lark who was leaning over the front seat squinting in the rearview mirror while she reapplied her lipstick for the hundredth time.

"Why are you doing that?" I asked. "Nobody can see you."

"Hey, loverboy," Andy yelled. "What's taking you so long?"

That really ticked me off, and I decided to take off on my own. It was awkward stuffing a leaflet under a windshield when your hands were full and, of course, I dropped my pile which flew all over the parking lot and under cars. As I stooped down to make a half-hearted attempt to pick them up, Lark scrambled behind me and started grabbing them like a maniac. "Just leave them there," I said. "Who cares . . ."

"Gene, pick those up!" Mom yelled from the street where she was leafleting the stray cars.

"Your mother," Lark said, "cares." She started laughing and the whole thing was so stupid I started laughing too. Between the two of us, we got most of them except for the ones that would've involved crawling under cars.

"I have an idea," Lark said, "for a system. You skate fast and throw a document on the hood of each car. I'll follow and tuck them under the wipers."

"Okay," I agreed. It was a lot better than my idea, which was to follow Corinne and Andy and take off all the ones they'd already done. I grabbed the pile of paper and went for it, skating from car to car in the darkness.

I finished just before Corinne and Andy. "Hey, losers," I yelled. "Superior skating and intellect win out as usual."

"You're not done," Corinne pointed out as they finished. "Lark's still putting them under wiper blades."

"So. They're on the cars." We skated up to each other to continue our argument while I ignored Lark asking for help in the background.

"Does it really matter who wins?" Mom butted in and spoiled things.

"It does tomorrow," I pointed out. Then I skated over to help Lark, who had started to send me pissed-off death rays.

"True," Mom admitted, following to help us. "It really really matters who wins the election."

We skated past midnight through the hills of Prospect Park lit by my mom slowly following in the car. We got rid of fifty to sixty more leaflets, getting possibly fifty to sixty more votes. That night I dumped the rest of them on my bedroom floor as a souvenir. I picked one up and finally looked at it. There was a picture of Paul Wellstone standing in the sun, smiling, next to the words VOTE TODAY. "I did it," I told Paul Wellstone. "I helped you win."

The next morning, my mom sat at the kitchen table with bloody hands. "Gross," Lily pointed out as Mom wrapped her hand in a paper towel and carefully picked up her mug of coffee.

"What happened?" I asked.

"Our sign." She didn't even have to say which one out of the dozens of signs that had crowded our front yard all fall. We all knew it must be the big Wellstone one. "Someone vandalized it. They pulled it out of the ground and ripped it in half." She peeled off the paper towel and winced. Her hands resembled raw meat— something cool on a skater but creepy on your own mom. "I may have ripped up my hands but at least I got those big stakes back in the ground and I taped the sign together."

"Why didn't you get me?" Dad asked. "I could've helped."

"I was too pissed off," Mom told him. Lily and I exchanged looks. My mom never said the word pissed. At the most, she was "frustrated" or "disappointed."

"You'd better put something on those," Dad advised.

"I'll kiss them for you," Lily offered.

"Like your spit would really help," I said.

"No time," Mom said. "I've got to vote before work."

At school, Lark and Corinne still had traces of Midnight Magic. When they walked from their lockers, I saw them in my mind coming at me from out of the dark, the street lights haloing them. Corinne bragged in Mr. Mac's class about meeting Walter Mondale the night before. Of course, Derrick Martin said, "So what. I've met Norm Coleman." Mr. Mac just beamed.

After class, I thought about how it was probably Derrick Martin who destroyed our Wellstone sign. As Andy and I walked past him, I said, "Can Norm Coleman hit this hard?" and slugged him in the arm just like Walter Mondale slugged Andy, but hopefully a lot harder.

"Hey!" he said as Andy and I raced away, laughing.

That night, the four of us went with my dad to the campaign party to celebrate our win. It was in this hotel in downtown St. Paul that was probably fancy a decade before I was born, but at that point looked worn out and faded. They gave us buttons that said, "WE ARE PAUL WELLSTONE," which Andy pointed out was kind of weird. "My girlfriend is Paul Wellstone?" He fake shuddered.

"Shut up!" said Corinne, who, in her usual tight jeans and top, didn't look anything like Paul Wellstone.

There were a lot of college students there so it felt good to belong. We joked around with each other while my dad talked to his friends. At first it felt like a good time, but we started noticing that even though it was noisy, we were the only ones laughing. Maybe it was just the bad florescent lighting, but it felt like the hyper-infusion of energy from the night before had fizzled out. Instead there was this negative vibe coming from the TVs perched at the top of the room. They were emitting this bluish gloom that was hanging over everyone.

"What's happening?" Corinne asked. "What is everybody's problem?"

"We're behind," Lark said.

"That's not possible," said Corinne. "We have to win."

"It's still early," I said. "They don't know anything yet. The votes from the Iron Range aren't in."

Dad walked up to us shaking his head. "We might as well go. The party's over. Now it's just the memorial service they wanted us to have."

"Mondale lost?" Andy asked.

Dad shrugged. "Mondale, and practically every Democrat on the ticket."

"You've got to be kidding," Corinne said.

We followed Dad out of the hotel. It was like Paul Wellstone had just died all over again.

Going to school the next day would've been bad anyway but it was a hundred times worse having to face the gloating of Derrick Martin. He spent the hour in Mr. Mac's class going on and on about how this was such a victory for the overtaxed and how the Republican guy who was just elected governor was an awesome hockey player. I wanted to get away from him but he followed me out into the hall and grabbed me by the shoulder. "Hey, Gene," he said, "I noticed your button." He poked the "We Are Paul Wellstone" button pinned to my hoodie. "*You* are Paul Wellstone?" He laughed. "What does that mean? That you're dead?"

Some jerk from *The Planet of the Apes* asks you something that's not only lame and rude, but puts into words exactly what you've been wondering yourself. What do you do?

A. Say, "Why, yes, that's what it means" and thank him for his brilliant insight.

B. Stand there and smile pathetically because after all, he won so he can do whatever he wants and since you lost, you just have to take it.

C. Remember you have another button that says "STAND UP KEEP FIGHTING." Let him snort until the snot runs out of his nose and he's rubbery with laughter, while all of the frustration at the unbelievable unfairness of everything builds inside you until finally it has to come out and you pull back your fist and let him have it.

Chapter Fourteen

Poop in a Blender Revisited

Sitting on the bench outside the vice-principal's office was something I'd never done before. The secretaries ignored me. Derrick Martin came from the nurse's office holding a giant cold pack to his face. I cheered up at the sight of him, wondering if I broke his nose. Then I realized that the secretaries were avoiding me like I was the kind of kid who'd bring a gun to school. I looked down at my shirt and noticed there was blood sprayed all over it.

I stared down at my shirt while Derrick met with Mr. Flink. I started feeling bad that I hadn't just walked away from Derrick. Like I had done, and should have gotten credit for having done, for the past ten years. Finally, Mr. Flink escorted Derrick out of his office. Derrick adjusted his cold pack and moaned for his audience of secretaries. They moaned back in sympathy and he gave me this self-satisfied little smile as he walked past.

The vice-principal's office was a cell made from cinder-block covered with posters of plastic-looking kids playing sports with lame slogans like "Team Players Are Winners" and "To Score a Goal You Have to Have One." For some reason, this reminded me that South was designed by a guy who usually designed prisons. It made me wonder if the vice in vice-principal referred to vice squad. Then he shook my hand, and I realized that vice described his grip.

"So tell me what happened, Eugene," said Mr. Flink, who looked at me with these eyes that looked like pebbles stuck in his doughy face.

"Umm. Derrick wouldn't let up about how the Democrats lost the election," I mumbled, trying to avoid his creepy eyes.

"So punching someone in the nose is the correct response to them taunting you?" he said.

"No," I mumbled. *Yes*, I thought.

"What is the correct response?" he asked, looking hard at me until I met his eyes.

"Ignore him," I said. *Punch him in the mouth so he couldn't tell his stupid lies.*

"What have you learned from this experience?" He leaned toward me, and I inched backwards.

"Umm," I said.

"Well?" His eyes became even harder and colder.

"I'm sorry I did it, and I'll never do it again," I fake apologized.

He didn't look convinced. "How?" he asked. "How will you avoid doing something like this again?"

"Avoid Derrick?" I said, which was the first honest answer I'd given. Mr. Flink narrowed his eyes so they looked like pencil lead. "Give myself a time-out," I said, reading the poster behind him that had a picture of two guys arguing on a basketball court above a picture of one of them going to the bench.

"Exactly!" he said and started this rant about living your life like you were playing a sport. He'd sat with his back to this poster for so long he probably didn't have a clue that everybody who gave him the answer he wanted was just reading it to him.

When I got home, our front yard looked deserted, like my family had moved away. It was the signs. All of the signs from the election were suddenly gone, including the Wellstone billboard. This made me so sad I could hardly stand it.

My whole family was sitting on the couch waiting for me under the patched up Wellstone sign that was now nailed to our living room wall. They might as well have put up a sign for the world to see that said "LOSERS AND PROUD OF IT."

Mom told Lily she should go play in her room for a while. Lily didn't even argue with her, which let me know I was in big trouble. Mom was really pissed off. Not that she said that. She said, "Gene, I'm so disappointed that you would do something like this." Of course, Derrick told everyone I had hit him the day before too.

"It was a friendly punch in the arm."

"Like that friendly punch in the nose?" Dad asked.

"Your father and I need to discuss your punishment," Mom said. Her face was pinched like I had caused her great pain.

"They already suspended me from school for three days," I pointed out.

"I suppose you think that's a reward." Mom's voice got louder and her face got red. She was mad and out of control. I guess it ran in the family.

Dad, at least, tried to be reasonable. "He does want to go to school," he said. "Maybe that and the fact that he'll always have this suspension on his record is enough."

The thought of this suspension on my permanent record like a felony really got my mom going. "I think we need to look at where this all started."

Dad and I both waited.

"Rollerblading," she announced.

"What?" I said. "What does skating have to do with Derrick Martin who's just a di–wiener anyway?"

Dad gave me this look like I'd better watch it or things were going to get worse—which they did.

"Skating was the reason you skipped school. That's when the trouble started."

"True," Dad said. He was always on her side.

"The trouble started when I worked on the campaign," I said. The only advice of Paul Wellstone's I seemed to be able to follow was to get into trouble. "Maybe you should keep me away from politics."

"You need to give us your skates, Gene," Mom said. "No more skating this year." Dad nodded in agreement.

"I can't," I said. My parents looked confused.

"Gene," Mom said. "You don't have a choice. Go get your Shimas now."

I went to my bedroom and threw myself on my bed.

You're already in trouble for one thing that wasn't totally your fault, although you are the only one in the entire universe who sees it that way, and now you're about to really get in trouble for something else that really wasn't totally your fault although everything you say in the next few minutes will definitely be held against you. What do you do?

A. Never speak again. What you don't say can't hurt you.
B. Never stop talking. Just go with anything that pops into your head like aliens and skate-eating raccoons until they get so worried about the problem of your missing brain, they forget all about any skates that may be missing.
C. Tell the truth. Then jump out the window.

After a while I heard my dad calling me, but I didn't answer. I just put my pillow over my head. Finally, my parents stood next to me.

"What's the big deal Gene?" Dad asked. "It's not like we're going to take them forever."

"You can't take them," I said into my pillow.

"What?" Mom said. "That's ridiculous. This is why we have to stop this obsession with skating. They're just skates, Gene."

"I don't have them anymore." Now the poop was really going to hit the blender.

"You want to explain that?" Dad asked, sitting on my bed.

"Not really." I hoped we could leave it at that, but, of course, we couldn't.

My mom and dad were so down on me, after I told them the story about Billy and the skates, I wondered if I should just move out and join Billy by the river. Maybe that was what drove him crazy—years of parental disapproval.

"They're just skates," I reminded my mom.

"They're skates that cost a lot of money," she pointed out.

"It was mostly my money." But it didn't seem to matter.

When I finally went back to school, it was like being released from solitary confinement. I'd only been allowed to leave my room to go to the bathroom and eat with my family. During meals, my parents obsessed about all the cuts in government programs the Republicans were going to make and about how Wellstone's memorial service, the only thing that had happened since the plane crash that wasn't depressing, was a huge mistake that cost us the election. It made me feel like I was wrong about everything. Not that it mattered. They chatted with Lily about little girl stuff, like I no longer existed. They didn't said anything more about a punishment. They let it hang over my head which should've been considered punishment enough if you had asked me.

At school, I did my best to avoid Derrick Martin. This was hard because, of course, there he was waiting for me in Mr. Mac's class first hour. I sat right up in front of Mr. Mac so Derrick couldn't talk to me. The class was boring. We'd moved on to the Constitution and Mr. Mac was moving in slow motion. He hardly asked for any class discussion and seemed careful about what he said, which wasn't entertaining at all. He'd even gelled his hair into submission. I didn't realize until he stopped me after class that it was all my fault.

"Mr. Snow," he said. "I've already talked with Mr Martin. I want to make it clear to both of you that the intent of my class is to learn about government and how it works. Not to sink to the level of talk radio."

"I know." I looked down at the floor. I still didn't feel bad I'd punched Derrick, but I did feel bad I must have gotten Mr. Mac in trouble. It was so unfair because he never took sides and he couldn't help it that Derrick Martin was somebody you just wanted to hit.

"I'd like you to think about this from Mr. Martin's perspective. It takes a lot of courage for him to express his views when he's in the minority."

"But . . ." I protested. It wasn't like Derrick Martin went around nobly expressing his views. He was an asshole.

"No buts," Mr. Mac interrupted. "I'm trying to think of a way to turn this into a learning experience."

Oh, no. I didn't know how many more of those learning experiences I could handle.

"You don't seem very enthusiastic," he observed.

You don't either, I wanted to say. Instead I told him, "Sorry," and hoped that he got that I was sorry about everything.

"I should have this figured out by next week," he said. "I'll let you know."

"Sure." I guessed I deserved whatever he decided since I had ruined AP Government for the rest of the year.

I didn't admit this to anyone else though. Instead I complained to Andy and Corinne about my parents. "Wouldn't you think three days of solitary confinement would be enough?"

Andy shrugged. "You hit him pretty hard. He looks bad."

Derrick did look bad. His face looked like the Northern Lights with all these green bruises streaking across it.

"I would've broken his nose," Corinne said. "He deserves it."

At least Lark was treating me like a hero. "Hey, Gene," she said, as she, Brady, and I all tried to take stuff out and cram stuff in to our shared locker simultaneously. Now that it was colder out, she was using teenage girl logic and wearing less than usual: a short plaid skirt, fishnet stockings and a sleeveless shirt. She was looking more and more like a typical South High student.

"Gene, could you punch this stinky boy in the nose for me?" She made a face at Brady. "I am disgusted with how he's ruining my stuff."

Brady made a face back at her. "Fine, Frenchy." All of my friends called Lark Frenchy even though she wasn't from France. Especially because she wasn't from France. They liked how it pissed her off, or as she said, "infuriated" her. "I'd just get blood and snot and pus all over your fancy stuff," Brady told her.

Lark frowned. I could tell she wanted to flip through her Dutch-to-English dictionary.

"Mucus," I interpreted. "And pus is—"

"I know what pus is!" she interrupted. Brady and I both laughed.

"I should punch both of you in the nostrils," she hissed and stalked past us.

"I wonder if she thinks pus is semen?" Brady said, which made us laugh even harder.

I didn't feel like laughing at home. My parents had finally figured out a punishment. It was like they'd forgotten about me punching Derrick, and they didn't even care about my skates anymore. Instead they were all focused on my bad attitude toward the homeless.

"I was nice to Billy," I protested. "I built the fence with him, and the reason he took my skates in the first place was that I was worried about him and checked on him."

"You threw fireworks at what was essentially his home," Mom said.

"I didn't do it."

"Who did?" Dad asked.

"I dunno." I wasn't going to rat out my friends.

"Since you're not going to tell us who did that horrible thing to Billy even though they obviously need help and since you didn't do the right thing and stop them in the first place, you need to do something that helps you understand how serious this is," Mom said.

I sighed. I was ready to do about anything she said just so she'd stop lecturing me.

"We've arranged for you to volunteer at Loaves and Fishes." She announced this like she'd found the cure for juvenile delinquency.

"With Sister Jude?" I really missed my skates, but I didn't miss Sister Jude.

"I've signed you up to do regular shifts on your own and then we've decided to do some as a family," Mom announced.

I groaned and looked at my dad. I knew Mom didn't have a clue, but this was a punishment for him, too. He wasn't exactly a do-gooder. He was more of an abstract kind of guy.

The next day, I found out my punishment—learning experience—from Mr. Mac. He told Derrick and me to stay after class. At least it felt good to hear Derrick whining that this was unfair because he didn't hit anyone.

Mr. Mac ignored him and told us he had a project he wanted the two of us to do together. "Together?" we both said.

"No way," Derrick said. And for the first time in my life, I found myself agreeing with him.

"I want you to do your History Day project together. This year's theme is conflict resolution, which seems appropriate to your situation." Mr. Mac rubbed his hands together getting all revved up. "Just think of the possibilities." It did feel good to see him get excited about something again.

"Fine," said Derrick. I agreed. I could tell he was thinking what I was. We could each work separately. Then stick our halves together.

"I'll plan to meet with you on a regular basis." Mr. Mac, of course, could read our minds. "To make sure you're working together. You know, you're my two top students, and I think you can go to state with this."

Derrick and I just looked at him. Both of us felt pretty pleased with ourselves to be one of Mr. Mac's two top students and pretty disgusted at who the other one was.

"But . . ." I said.

"No buts." Mr. Mac bounced up from his chair. "Mr. Martin, Mr Snow." He shook our hands. "It'll be a pleasure to work with you."

As we walked out, I noticed one positive thing. Derrick Martin was avoiding me.

CHAPTER FIFTEEN

H-E-DOUBLE HOCKEY STICKS

Lark was mad at me. Not pouty-mouthed cute mad. More like thin-lipped, arms folded across her chest, waiting for an answer I couldn't give mad.

"You and Brady were making fun of me," she accused. The color of her lipstick reminded me of the red ink teachers use to correct papers.

"Brady always makes fun of you."

"You don't have to join in."

"I'm sorry." I tried to put my arm around her, which was like trying to put your arm around the Ice Queen. "Sometimes I can't help it," I added. "You're funny."

Then she turned into Dragon Lady and practically breathed fire on me. "I'd like to see you speak fluently in another language. I've heard you practice your sick Spanish. You suck."

I stepped back at that. That wasn't a word she learned from her Dutch-to-English dictionary.

Thankfully, Corinne and Andy walked by and distracted us. As Lark said hi, I noticed Corinne was looking good in her latest Alicia Keyes meets the Ramones outfit. Andy was grinning.

"There you are. Doing it again." Lark blasted back into my consciousness as they walked away.

"What?"

"You were looking. You are always looking at her."

"Who?" I asked, because if I let on that I knew who she was talking about she'd probably start hitting me with her cosmetic stuffed purse and swearing at me in a foreign language.

"Corinne. My best friend and your best friend's girlfriend." She looked like she was going to cry, and it finally occurred to me—okay, I was just a dumb male—that this was what she was really mad about.

"I was also looking at Andy," I said in my defense. "Why doesn't it bother you that I look at Andy?"

"Because Andy is not a gorgeous skater girl!" Lark yelled over the ten thousand decibels of hall noise.

Brady walked up just as she stalked off.

"What'd I do now?" He inflated his scrawny chest like he was proud of his repulsive powers.

"Nothing. It was me. I looked at Corinne."

Brady shook his head, which set his black cloud of hair in motion. "Dude, everybody looks at Corinne."

I considered following Lark and telling her this but somehow I didn't think it would help my case. "Yeah, but they look at Lark too," I said.

"I guess so." Brady shrugged and his thunderstorm of hair changed directions. "Until they get to know her."

That afternoon, I sacked out on the couch and discussed my troubles with my therapist, my therapy dog, Dr. Yellow.

"I've been looking at Corinne all school year," I complained. "Why does Lark have to get mad about it now?"

Yellow groaned either in sympathy or because I pushed him away when he tried to scramble up on the couch with me.

"You know," I said, petting him and giving him a potato chip, "I've got enough stress having to spend most of my free time with that asshole Derrick Martin and that witch Sister Jude. If you had to waste what's supposed to be the best time of your life with those two, you'd look at girls too."

Yellow gave me his sad-eyed dog look. "I wish I could do that," I told him. I held off giving him another chip just so I could figure out how he was so effective. "If I looked at Lark like that, I bet I could get away with anything."

Yellow lunged at the potato chip bag, but I held it up in the air. "I'm not saying you can get away with everything, you dumb dog." I tossed a chip across the room so he had to run for it.

Maybe Lark got mad because she really did think pus was semen. She'd probably overheard Brady brag about what he'd do with a girl if he ever got near one. Maybe Corinne talked to her about what she and Andy did. I didn't know what girls talked about. I didn't want to know.

Lark told me once that she took birth control pills and before I could stop myself, I'd blurted out, "Why?"

"For my complexion," she said. "I just thought you'd want to know."

"Uh thanks." I didn't know what I was supposed to say.

"I've never had to take them for contraception." She blushed.

"Neither have I," I admitted. "Not that a guy takes . . . well, you know what I mean."

Anyway, I wasn't sure if I felt better she wasn't as sophisticated as she appeared or worse because she expected me to be more sophisticated. Usually when my friends started talking about having sex, Andy just smiled to himself and we were left to our imaginations. I tried to copy his expression and hoped I could keep getting away without saying anything. Usually, either Brady or Sam took over with their bragging.

Sam, the ladies man, would be in big trouble if girls ever heard what he said behind their backs. Brady was full of shit but he was pretty entertaining.

When my family finally came home, Mom reminded me that our family was going to Loaves and Fishes.

Dad, who was not thrilled at the prospect of doing good with the nuns, grumbled, "I didn't know it was tonight. I've got work to do."

"Your job is to set a good example," Mom pointed out, which stopped him from complaining, but then he started asking questions.

"Do we eat there?"

"I think so," Mom said doubtfully.

"Probably not." I was the voice of experience, remembering how stingy that nun was with the lemonade. "That would be wasting their food."

"I guess we should eat a snack before we go, but we're running late," Mom said.

We ended up sharing my bag of potato chips as we walked down the street.

"Why does this have to be so complicated?" Lily wailed. "I'm starving."

"Look," Mom lectured. "We're not going to be very helpful if we don't get our act together. Right now we're acting like—"

"The dysfunctional family from Hell?" Dad suggested.

"H-E- double hockey sticks," Lily corrected him.

When we got to the convent, we went to the side door, walking past the few old guys that came early. Dad glanced back at the fence. "Nice design. You did a good job on that, Gene."

Dad seemed to be working hard to accept things that usually annoyed him. When we got downstairs, I noticed he bowed his head in prayer when the nuns said grace although I knew he thought even Unitarians were too religious. I wasn't bowing my head. I was sneaking a peek around the room to see if Billy was there. But if he was he was keeping a low profile.

It turned out that after standing at a counter, dishing out mashed potatoes, mystery meat and canned peas, we were allowed to eat. The catch was we had to sit with these bad-smelling people. We joined these old guys in Army fatigues who stunk like beer and cigarettes. Lily looked like she was going to say something embarrassing. But then my mom whisked her off to another table to rescue a mom with a whole bunch of kids who were losing it.

Unfortunately, this left my dad and me to carry the conversation at the bums' table. I had to give Dad credit for trying. He asked them what they did. This was kind of risky because chances were they didn't do anything. A couple of guys surprised me and talked about how they worked jobs that didn't pay enough to live anywhere but the streets. I wondered how could you be expected to work all day and sleep in a cardboard box at night? I'd quit and rob banks or something. I'd use the money to start my own Loaves and Fishes. But instead of that rubbery mystery meat I'd serve steak. Loaves and Steak.

For dessert we had these neon green cupcakes that looked like they were radioactive. At Loaves and Steak, I'd serve birthday cake with tons of good frosting instead of stuff that tasted like toothpaste. I'd serve it every night because it was usually somebody's birthday. Sister Jude joined us just as I choked down my cupcake. I was actually glad to see her because, after we exhausted the topics of minimum wage and the weather, no one had said a word for about ten minutes. Dad seemed glad to see her too. But he didn't know any better.

"So," she said. "How was your meal?"

We all grunted in approval. Except for Dad who said, "Very good." I noticed he'd passed on the cupcakes.

Then she started asking the bums questions about their families, their fights with welfare, their aches and pains like she really knew them. It was weird because I had to work so hard to be good enough for her and they already were. "Has anyone seen Billy?" she asked.

She asked the one question that was on my mind. Unfortunately, these guys just clammed up.

"Eugene." Dad looked surprised when she used my formal name. "Can I see you outside for a minute?"

"Sure," I said, hoping I could miss clean up.

I followed Sister Jude up the stairs through the dark sanctuary. She opened the big front door, sat down on the steps and, of course, took out a cigarette. Besides keeping the skaters out, the fence around the stairs made a nice private place for her to smoke.

"Eugene." She lit her cigarette and closed her eyes as she took a long addicted drag. "I need your help."

I sighed. Why wasn't it enough to build this fence, put up with Billy and serve and eat this lousy food? Sister Jude was starting to remind me of Paul Wellstone—minus the charisma—with her high expectations and my irrational need to please her.

"I need you to find Billy for me." She looked at me with her worried eyes which were ringed by wrinkles.

"But . . ."

"He took your skates, which has to mean something to him in his crazy universe. He needs to get back on his medication before he gets into trouble. You're the only one who can find him."

This insane nun who has accepted you as her personal savior asks you to do something you know is beyond your nonexistent powers. What do you do?

140

A. **Agree to find Billy because what the H-E-double hockey sticks, it's the only way you're going to get your skates back and get Sister Jude to leave you alone.**
B. **Ask her why does she care so much about Billy? What makes him more special than all the other bums? Point out that she doesn't seem to care that much if they go off their medications. Point out maybe she's the one who needs to go on medication.**
C. **Realize that it doesn't really matter what you agree to because you don't have a chance in H-E-double hockey sticks of finding him or your long lost Shimas.**

"But . . ." I gave up. "Fine."

"God bless you, Eugene." I had to get up before she did something creepy like try to hug me.

Our family finally walked back home and everyone seemed glad to have that experience behind them. Then I remembered this wasn't a one shot deal. "How often did you sign us up to do this?" I asked my mom. Dad, Lily, and I all held our breath waiting for the answer.

"I signed you up once a week and our family once a month for the rest of the year."

That wasn't too bad. It was almost Thanksgiving so it would only be a month and a half. Dad looked relieved.

"The school year. Not the calendar year," Mom clarified.

"That's until summer!" Lily whined. "This is going to be H-E-double hockey sticks."

"Lily!" I wasn't sure if Mom was shocked by her bad language or her bad attitude.

Dad and I both agreed with Lily. We'd do it but we didn't have to pretend it was easy.

The next day at school was about as socially stimulating as sitting at the bums' table. For some reason, no one talked to me. I tried to talk to Lark after Government but she walked away. Then I caught up with Andy and Corinne but Corinne ignored me and kept talking to Andy. Andy just gave me this look like I was a bad dog and he wasn't allowed to play with me.

As the bell rang, I forced myself to swallow my pride and asked Derrick Martin when he wanted to get together to work on our History Day project.

"Got a lot of time on your hands now that Lark dumped you?" He smirked. "Sure, I'll come over to your house after supper."

Lark dumped me? I knew she was mad at me but she never said she dumped me. Was that how it worked? I'd never been dumped before.

When I walked home with Brady, he said how glad he was that I'd finally come to my senses. "You two made me sick. I could hardly stand to go to my locker."

I didn't know what was worse: being dumped and having to be grateful to Derrick Martin for pointing it out or listening to my friend tell me my former girlfriend was a loser. Even though Lark wasn't Corinne, I still liked her. She could have at least had the decency to tell me herself. But apparently that wasn't how these things were done. I figured I was just supposed to accept that I couldn't talk to her anymore or anyone who decided to be her friend.

This, of course, brought me to Andy. I couldn't believe he chose Lark over me. Well, that wasn't really true, he chose Corinne. I didn't know what I'd do if I were in his place. I'd never been in that place even though I had to admit I tried to get there.

I kind of had a stomach ache during supper which was weird because there was no mystery meat or green cupcakes to blame it on. Then I remembered Derrick was coming over.

"Do we have to have that sign up in the living room?" I asked as I cleared my plate.

"What sign?" Mom said, because for her it wasn't a sign anymore. It was part of our house.

"The Wellstone sign. It's kind of embarrassing."

"Embarrassing?" Mom stopped putting leftovers away and looked at me like I was the one who was crazy.

"Derrick Martin's coming over tonight."

"Good. You're starting your project?"

"Yeah," I said. "But the Wellstone sign. Couldn't we just take it down for the night? It's kind of a distraction."

"Sounds like a teachable moment," my mom, the teacher said. "The point of you and Derrick working together is that it's okay for you to have different viewpoints."

"Yeah, but it's your viewpoint," I pointed out.

"What do you mean? You're not a Wellstone supporter?"

"I just want to have a normal living room with pictures of nature and stuff."

Then Dad got involved. "We have never had a normal living room with pictures of nature and stuff. And we never will."

"And we will never take down our Wellstone sign." Mom got all emotional. "Ever."

So this was my punishment, I realized as I invited Derrick Martin in to humiliate me. I was sure his house looked just like it did when we were the only two losers from the neighborhood who got stuck in the other kindergarten class and I had to go over there for playdates. I could've guaranteed his house had pictures of flowers and lake scenes on the walls, not campaign signs or bizarre UAO's—unidentifiable art objects.

We walked past the Wellstone sign, which I knew he saw but didn't acknowledge. His parents had probably given him a lecture to be on his best behavior. Maybe he was the one who wrecked it which, at least, would've motivated him to keep his mouth shut. We went up to my room and sat at my computer checking websites. I wanted to do the Middle East Peace Process but Derrick said no because the Democratic president, Jimmy Carter was involved.

I said, "How about Northern Ireland?" Of course we checked it out and found all this stuff about George Mitchell, another Democrat. "Look," I told Derrick, "if we find out that all the great historical conflicts were resolved by Democrats you're just going to have to pick one."

"This is why Democrats are such asswipes," Derrick said. "They think they're the ones going around solving the world's problems when, in actuality, they're just the ones taking credit."

We were about to start another conflict ourselves when we hit on the idea of Nelson Mandela and South African reconciliation.

"I think we've got to do something about how someone did this impossible thing that no one thought they could do," Derrick said. "This guy was in prison for twenty seven years and then he becomes president of South Africa. Why didn't he shrivel up and die or get out and kill someone?"

"Yeah," I admitted. "I wonder how he did it." I thought about my three days in solitary confinement, about all the impossible things I wanted to do. About how everything had seemed impossible in my house since Paul Wellstone died and we'd lost the election.

"Strategy," Derrick said. "You have to get into your opponent's mind and figure out how they think."

"Empathy." My mom interrupted us with a plate of cookies. "Isn't it just putting yourself in another person's place and imagining how you'd feel?"

I gave her a look that said, "Go away. You are causing me great pain and embarrassment," but Derrick thanked her for the cookies and took what she had said seriously. "I don't know, Mrs. Snow. That's too hard to do. If I feel anything for anybody I usually just feel sorry for them."

"Empathy is hard," she empathetically agreed.

"Yeah," said Derrick. Then when Mom left the room he looked at me and added under his breath. "Like you. I feel really sorry for you."

CHAPTER SIXTEEN
WILD MAN

I thought a lot about what Derrick had said about getting into your opponent's mind. Since I was pretty much a friendless loser, I had a lot of time and opponents to think about. For one thing, even though he wasn't my enemy, I'd started looking at Mr. Mac differently. I wasn't as intimidated by him. He'd met with me and Derrick every Thursday for the past month since we'd started our project and got really excited about our research. He kept jumping up from his chair and asking us questions. I was pretty sure he had ADHD and channeled all his excess energy into teaching. I used to think he spazzed out to get our attention, but maybe he just couldn't help it.

I thought about Andy. How smart he was and how I'd always had to work to keep up with him. I wondered what he got on the PSAT. I got my results and did pretty well. "Because you studied," Mom said. I was sure Andy did better.

I also thought about Lark and how she must have hated me. This was easy since we still shared a locker. Even though we did a pretty good job of figuring out when the other one wouldn't be there, at least once a day we accidentally ran into each other. I tried to say hi, when what I wanted to tell her was "I'm sorry I ever acknowledged the existence of Corinne, who can't measure up to you in terms of being knowledgeable, extremely articulate in a second language and a tight European dresser." I tried to imply all that when I said hi, but it didn't matter because she didn't acknowledge my existence.

She talked to Brady and was even nice to him. One day she said, "Brady, thank you for moving your garbage off the top shelf," as she put a book up there, turning it so I couldn't read the title.

"That was my lunch," Brady explained. "I ate it."

I laughed but she ignored me.

I didn't even try to talk to Andy or Corinne. And I didn't even look at Corinne. I saw myself as everyone must have seen me. Some pervert ogling his best friend's girlfriend.

As far as I could figure out, I only had one hope and his name was Billy. I'd been trying to enter my opponent Billy's mind, which was hard because I couldn't figure out how he thought, especially if he was off his medication. But I knew if I could find Billy and get my skates back, I could enter the skate competition that spring, win it and Corinne and Lark would fight over me. Andy would be able to get over Corinne because he'd have me back as a best friend. Maybe he needed some time without a girlfriend anyway. Maybe he needed to have Brady tell him how sick he was of his sickening behavior.

In the meantime, I still had to practice even though the weather sucked and my parents wouldn't let me skate at an indoor park. They hadn't banned Nintendo or DVDs though so I started studying. I played Nintendo Aggressive Inline. I skated "the edge of sanity" as the cover said and skated as all the top skaters, including Chris Edwards. I knew I was just pushing buttons but it helped me get into it. Then I studied Chris Edwards's video *Dare to Air* and DVDs of Louie Zamora and Dre Powell, the guy Corinne said I skated like. Watching Dre Powell made me realize Corinne did think I was good. He had this fluidity. If Louie Zamora was a crazy man, Dre Powell was an artist.

One night I headed to the rink at the park just after they turned off the overhead lights. My parents never said I wasn't allowed to ice skate and it felt good just to mess around. I skated in the purple dark. I did manual stuff—not high-end skating. Stuff like skating on my toes like they were two front wheels. I jumped off hockey boards, did 360s over some trashed hockey sticks. I copied Dre Powell. Tried to master his cess slide, which was a thing of beauty. On ice skates it was just a hockey stop, which made me realize the only thing that had been holding me back was a little cement and wheels.

I did wild and crazy jumps even though I knew if I landed wrong and broke my leg or neck, no one knew I was there. I probably would've laid there and froze to death. Once in a while I felt someone watching. It was probably wishful thinking. I imagined Billy sliding across the ice, handing me my Shimas, saying "Here, looks like you need these."

Over Christmas break, I went down to the river wondering if Billy could survive there in the cold. It was totally deserted. His camp was covered in snow like it had never been there. I walked farther down to the water and wondered if he was even still alive, imagining his body floating while my skates had sunk to the bottom. But it didn't feel like Billy was dead. It felt like he was waiting for me somewhere, surprised it was taking me so long to find him.

Every week in the musty church basement, I asked about Billy. The old guys' table was used to me asking by now. I'd say, "Has anyone seen Billy? He's a vet, has a ponytail, builds things?"

Every week the same guys grunted in response. The same guys who never said anything didn't say a word and this one guy, Schwartz, piped up as usual, "Vet, long hair, builds things? . . . Nope, haven't seen him."

That week, I didn't bother saying anything. Finally Schwartz asked, "Eugene, did you ever find your friend Billy?"

"No, " I said. Everybody sat there waiting. It was like they couldn't eat until we went through the routine. Kind of like how they waited for the nuns to say grace. "Have you seen him?" I forced myself to ask. I was so tired of it: the bad smells, the unappetizing food, the boring conversations.

"Vet, ponytail, builds things, has a pair of roller skates sticking out of his pack?" Schwartz asked.

"Skates!" I'd never told them about my skates. "You've seen him? Where?"

"Maybe," Schwartz said. "Maybe I've seen him."

A couple of the guys who never talked, nodded their heads. And the other old guys said, "Yup."

Then a guy, who usually just shoveled in the food, said,"Wild Man!"

The other guys agreed. "Wild Man. That man is wild!"

"What does he do—fight?" I asked. "Where have you seen him?"

"Lots of guys fight," Schwartz said. "He has this wild look in his eyes. You know, like if he did fight, he'd kill you."

"Where?" I asked again, worried they might stop talking or change the subject.

"Shelter," someone said.

"Downtown," Schwartz added.

"You guys are great," I told them. They nodded and grunted and dug into their food. When I passed out dessert, I offered them seconds when the nuns weren't looking. They all took more cookies, even though they were stale and tasted like sawdust.

When Sister Jude insisted I sit with her and inhale her secondhand smoke, I expected her to, as usual, interrogate me about Billy. Instead she said with this self-satisfied look, "I have a project for us, Eugene."

Oh, no, I thought. I knew Sister Jude meant well in her efforts to save the world, but did she have to screw up everything in my life as she did it?

"I've been asked to speak at a peace rally. To talk about things from the vets' perspective."

"That's nice," I said, wondering how this would make my life miserable.

"I thought we could do it together." She smiled like she was pleased with herself. "There's going to be a lot of students there, and I want to appeal to them. We make a good team, don't you think?"

"I'm pretty busy," I said, imagining the humiliation of having to do what Sister Jude told me in front of a crowd of my former and soon to be former friends. What if she made me pray in front of them?

"I'll give it to you as soon as I'm done writing it." I winced as she ground her cigarette into the steps.

"I can't . . ." I started to say but Sister Jude had never taken no for an answer.

"I've already discussed it with your mother. She's so proud of you."

Of course. The possibility of war had made my parents even crazier. We had a new yard sign that said, "Stop the Iraq War. Contact Your Congressperson." I told Derrick we had to meet at his house to work on our history day project because my family was sick, which was kind of true. Sister Jude smiled at me like she hoped it was contagious.

The next day after school, I decided I had another reason to find Billy. Maybe he'd be enough to distract Sister Jude. Maybe he could give that speech with her. It was about as realistic as me doing it. I tried looking up the downtown homeless shelter, but I couldn't get on the Internet because of some upgrade my dad was in the middle of and I'd left my cell phone in my locker.

I felt stuck and this made me really miss my friends. I hadn't told Sam or Brady about my search for Billy because they were the ones who attacked him in the first place. Corinne probably wouldn't have been much help, but Andy or Lark would've known what to do.

I picked up the phone and dialed Andy's number before I thought about why I shouldn't. A girl answered.

"Sorry, wrong number." I hung up as fast as I could. My phone rang.

"I know it's you, Snow, so don't even think about hanging up. Just what is your problem?"

"Corinne?" It took every ounce of willpower not to hang up, find the homeless shelter on my own and spend the rest of my miserable life there.

"I wasn't trying to call you," I tried to explain, knowing that in her eyes I was a pathetic teenage stalker. "I thought maybe Andy could help me with something."

"Well, he's not in now." She put on this receptionist voice. "And I'm taking his calls. How can I help you?"

"You can't," I blurted out before I remembered you should never tell Corinne she couldn't do something.

"I'm coming over." She hung up. So I sat there like an idiot, waiting for her.

When I let her in, I realized I could've at least gone upstairs and checked myself out in the mirror. Instead I was stuck looking like one of the leads in *Revenge of the Nerds*.

But Corinne didn't even bother to look at me. I was trying so hard not to look at her that when I did I could tell she thought that was all I was doing. She adjusted her shirt, adjusted her hair, cocked her head at an angle.

"Give me the phone," she demanded after I told her about trying to find Billy and my skates at the homeless shelter.

She turned away from me and said, "Hi, I've got a friend and it's kind of an emergency and he doesn't have anywhere to live." She walked away as I tried to grab the phone back. "Can you tell me where the downtown homeless shelter is?" She dug a pen out of her pack and wrote on her hand. "Thanks."

"You can't call 911 for something like that," I said. That was why I didn't want to get Corinne involved in the first place. She was a magnet for trouble. Look at all the trouble I was already in just for looking at her.

"That's what 911 is for," Corinne told me. "The lady was really nice to me."

"Why didn't you use your phone then?" I asked. "Or Andy's."

"Well, it's your problem isn't it? So we should use your phone." She called the number on her hand, still using my family's phone. "Give me your hand," she ordered, grabbing it.

Just then Mom and Lily walked in, happily chattering, their arms full of school stuff. I pulled my hand away but Corinne grabbed it back and started writing on it. Then she hung up and answered her own phone. Mom and Lily stood there watching us.

"I'll be right there," she said. "I was running an errand."

"Uh, thanks," I said, as she let go of my hand.

"I'll meet you there after school." She grabbed my hand again and copied the address onto her hand.

"Uh, okay," I said.

Mom interrupted, "Well, hello, Corinne. How are you?"

Corinne rattled off "Hi—sorry—got to go," picked up her stuff and headed out the door.

"What was that all about?" Mom asked.

"Nothing," I muttered and headed for my room before she asked anything else.

"Gene's going on a date." I heard Lily singsong as I walked up the stairs.

The next day after school, I took the bus straight downtown to the homeless shelter. I waited for Corinne, but the only people around were these guys hanging out on the street, who all wanted my almost nonexistent money. I finally gave up and went inside to talk to this guy at this desk. He looked up from his newspaper and told me to come back later because he wanted to make this perfectly clear—they were not a day shelter. "I don't need a place to stay," I told him. "I'm looking for someone."

"You see anyone here besides me?"

"Uh no," I said. "But I was wondering if you'd seen a guy named Billy—vet, pony tail, carries a pair of inline skates around."

"Sounds like every other guy we have coming in here." He turned back to his paper.

I sighed and walked out, letting the door slam behind me. "Asshole," I muttered. "Like everybody that comes here carries skates."

"Did you say skates?" This guy I was walking past asked.

"Yeah." I tried to catch a better view of him and his pack, wondering if maybe they did all have skates. "Schwartz!"

A bunch of bums gathered round me. "So you decided to look for Wild Man?" Schwartz asked. "Why did you ask him?"

He gestured toward the shelter entrance and the rest of the guys growled in agreement. "Wild Man's at the shelter."

"That's why I came here." I was getting irritated.

"This ain't the shelter," he explained and the rest of them laughed. "This is crap. They make you sleep on the floor here or in plastic chairs under office lights. Don't want you to get too comfortable. Just don't want to get blamed if you die."

"Oh," I said. I couldn't believe how bad these guys were treated. "Where is it then?"

"If you've got bus fare, I'll show you," Schwartz said.

I dug in my pockets but there was nothing left. "I gave it all away." I looked at the guys I gave it to. Nobody offered to give back anything. "Can we walk there?" I asked.

"We can walk and try to earn the fare as we go."

"How do we do that?"

"Panhandle."

"You need some money?" I turned to see Corinne. "Let's get going," she said, like I was the one who was late. "Where do we catch the bus?"

We took the bus across downtown while Corinne griped at me for not answering my phone. I didn't turn it on a lot at that point since nobody called me but my parents. I was concentrating so much on Corinne that I almost missed Schwartz getting off. "C'mon," I said, running after him.

He led us over this bridge, then under it. "Downtown shelter," he announced proudly. There were beer cans and whiskey bottles everywhere.

"There's no one here," I said. The river looked industrial, like a cold stream of toxic waste. It was easy to imagine a dead body floating in it.

"This place is scary." This was from Corinne, the girl who didn't like people to think she was afraid of anything.

Schwartz whistled, then smiled toothlessly at us. "Wait," he ordered. He disappeared through some bushes and didn't come back. No one came for a long time.

"Let's ditch him and get out of this place, " Corinne said. "Maybe he just brought us here to rob us."

"We don't have much money," I pointed out. "He knows that."

"Yeah, well maybe he forgot. He doesn't seem like he has the greatest memory. He almost ditched us on the bus."

"I want my skates back. You can leave if you want."

"Right. Like I'm going anywhere around here by myself."

We waited a while longer, then the bushes rustled. "Who's there?" Corinne asked.

"Billy?" I said. "Is that you?"

Billy walked out towards us looking like the cadaver I'd imagined at the river.

"Billy," I got right to the point. "Why did you take my skates?"

"Huh?" he said.

"Great." Corinne was exasperated but I wasn't done yet.

"Did you sell them? You could live off those skates for a long time if you live under a bridge. Right ?" Billy just stared at me and Corinne gave me a look like I was being stupid to give him ideas. "You wanted to punish me, didn't you? Like working on that fence with you wasn't punishment enough."

"Gene, you're being kind of weird," Corinne said.

"You just do really dumb things that get you in trouble and that leads to more trouble and then you have to have the nuns rescue you and now you think I'm going to just give up my skates without saying anything. Where are my skates?" My voice got louder.

"Dunno." Billy turned to leave.

"Wait a minute." I went after him and grabbed him, too frustrated to be afraid. "Where are my skates? I want my skates." I shook him. It was like shaking a skeleton.

He looked like he did when I first met him: jittery and wild. Like a creature that had been caught and was trying to get away. He opened his mouth and howled.

"Stop it!" Corinne yelled. I let go even though I didn't know which one of us she was talking to. I let go of Billy and any hope of ever getting my skates back.

Chapter Seventeen

Beautiful Beast

"Let's get outta here." Corinne tugged at my arm as I started to follow Billy into the bushes.

"I'm supposed to bring him back," I insisted and pulled away from her. "And I want my skates."

"He doesn't have them," she said, which stopped me cold.

"What? You don't know that." But I decided to follow her as she climbed up the river bank.

"Did you see them in his pack?" she asked, as we crossed the bridge.

"Uh, no," I admitted. I hadn't really noticed he'd had a pack at all.

She stopped as we got to the bus stop and put her hands on her hips. "You didn't notice his pack did you?" she accused. "You were too into your insane interrogation game. You're pretty psycho, Snow, no wonder no one wants to be around you." She tossed her hair back and glared at me.

We got on the bus. She payed. Great, this was the closest I'd ever get to going on a date with Corinne Camden: visiting a bum hangout, her treat, and getting to hear how she thought I was psycho.

"No way did he have your skates in his pack."

"What—do you have x-ray vision or something? They could have been hidden."

"There wasn't room." As she said this, I noticed there wasn't room on the bus seat for both of us and our packs. My leg was touching hers. "His pack would barely hold a pair of baby booties."

"He could have had them hidden at the bum camp," I said, still mad at myself for missing the chance to go after him.

"Did you really want a bunch of crazy guys to attack us? I don't know what's the matter with you. It's like you're used to them or something."

I was used to them. I spent more time with the bums at Loaves and Fishes and talked to them more than I did any of my former friends those days.

"Besides, I don't think he has them."

"Why?" Why couldn't somebody helpful have been helping me? Like Lark or Andy.

"Because if you'd stop giving him your asinine theories you would have noticed that he didn't know what you were talking about." Corinne inched her leg away from me.

"Oh. Don't you think that's because he's crazy?"

"You're the one who's crazy." She got up to get off the bus.

The next time at Loaves and Ishes as Lily called it, I told Sister Jude I'd found Billy. "Is he here?" she asked, starting to walk out of the kitchen to see him.

"I saw him last week." I watched her excitement turn to disappointment.

"Last week?" she said. "He could be anywhere by now."

"Oh." I hadn't thought of that. "Maybe not. I could take you there."

"The camp under the bridge?" she asked. "I've been there."

"You've been there?" Why the hell she did she need me to help her?

"He won't come out for me," she explained.

"He doesn't have my skates," I repeated Corinne's theory.

Sister Jude gave me this weird look, like all of the sudden she cared more about my skates than I did. "Of course he has your skates, Eugene, you just need to bring him back to me and I'll get them for you."

That night I trudged home, skateless as usual, full of fake mashed potatoes, creamed corn, and gravy. "Why is Sister Jude so weird about Billy?" I said as I walked in the door.

"Probably because he's her weirdo brother," Lily piped up from the living room.

"What?" I walked between her and the TV.

"Quiet," she said. "My show's on."

"Lily." I stood there. "What do you mean he's her brother?" The laugh track on her show got louder like what I just said was hilarious.

"He's her brother." Lily sounded exasperated. "Everybody knows that."

"I didn't know that. How do you know that?"

"Move!" she said. "It's my favorite part and I'm missing it." I stepped out of the way and collapsed on the couch. How could everybody have known that and not me? When a commercial came on, I grabbed the remote and pressed mute.

"Hey!" Lily protested. "That's my favorite commercial!"

"You've seen that commercial a hundred times."

"Mom!" she yelled.

Mom came in instead of lecturing us from another room like she usually did. "What's going on here?" she asked.

"Lily says that everybody knows Sister Jude is Billy's sister. Not nun type sister but his real sister."

"Really? I didn't know that." Mom tilted her head, considering this. "Guess it makes sense though. She seems so worried about him."

"How do you know that?" I asked Lily once more.

"I listen. Most of the time people don't even know I'm there. That's how I know everything," she bragged.

I pulled out my pack to start my homework. Why didn't Sister Jude ever tell me that Billy was her brother? If she knew where he was why didn't she just go and drag him out? How was I ever gonna get my math homework done? My head was so full of questions I had a headache.

The next morning, Lark followed me out of first hour and said, "Gene, I am apprehensive about the Government test. May I come over tonight and study with you?"

I stopped and looked at her like I'd seen a ghost, a ghost with pink lip gloss and really good hair. You couldn't stop in the halls at South. It was like stopping in the middle of the freeway during rush hour. I should've known, I'd done both. Somebody bumped into me and like a human domino I bumped into her. "Sorry." I bent down to pick up the notebook I knocked out of her hand. "Uh sure," I said, wondering was this really how it was done? They just got back together with you with no explanation at all like nothing had ever happened?

When Lark came over to study, my family was a little too happy to see her.

"Why, Lark," Mom said, "We've missed you around here."

"We've missed your chocolate," Dad added.

"I've missed you too," Lark said. "Especially Lily." She put her arm around my little sister, who smirked at me.

We sat at the dining room table. I'd put my stuff there before Lark came so we could avoid the awkwardness of the couch. I was so nervous about having her there that I opened my book and immediately started quizzing her. She, of course, knew everything and didn't really need to study. But we just kept working and going over everything, which had the effect of disappointing Lily, the eavesdropper.

We decided to reread a chapter and then go over it, but I was having a hard time concentrating. Lark had done something to her hair. It was the color of honey instead of that Barbie doll blonde. She smelled really good, as usual, but her makeup was different too, less dramatic. She looked less like a European model and more like a really hot teenage girl.

"What?" Lark looked up from her book.

"Nothing." I felt my face go red and looked down.

"You looked like you were going to say something."

Your ex-girlfriend who may not be the perfect one for you, but is this totally gorgeous girl who seems to be making an effort to be a real teenager instead of someone on the cover of _Elle_, gives you a chance, a chance to say just the right thing, the thing that will flush all the crap from the past down the toilet and let you start over again. What do you do?

A. Say "I was just noticing how beautiful you are," as you gaze sincerely into her eyes.

B. Say "I wanted to say I'm sorry. How could I have ever looked at anyone else when I could be looking at you," as you gaze sincerely into her eyes.

C. Don't say anything. Just gaze sincerely into her eyes and lean over and kiss her.

These, of course, were the options of someone more sophisticated than me. "Nothing," I looked away and muttered. "Well, I'd better get to work on my math homework," I added, still not daring to look at her.

"Oh," she said, in this hurt voice, and closed her book. "I guess I'd better be going then." She got up, put on her coat and headed for the door.

"Did you do something to your hair?" I blurted out as she was leaving.

"A while ago." She put her fingers through it self-consciously.

"I like it," I said. "It looks . . ." I paused trying to find just the right word . . ."nice."

"Oh." Her voice kind of quavered like she might start crying. Then she gave me this big lit-up smile. "Thanks."

She closed the door. I turned to find Lily there. "You really blew it," she said. "Don't you want her to be your girlfriend?"

The next day I found out that it wasn't up to me. Corinne and Andy were talking to me again, stopping by my locker which had once again become Lark's and mine.

"Did you get your skates back yet?" Corinne asked me.

"No," I said. I'd given up on my skates. All I wanted to do was to get out of Loaves and Fishes duty and avoid seeing Sister Jude for the rest of her twisted life.

During lunch, Corinne mentioned my skates again. "You know you should be practicing for the street comp this spring. You've got to get them back."

I took a deep breath and told Corinne, Lark, and Andy about finding Billy and finding out about Sister Jude, leaving out the part about Corinne because I got the distinct impression she had never mentioned her involvement to these guys. "So

162

I'm pretty sure Billy doesn't have my skates and I have no idea why Sister Jude lied to me," I told them.

"Doesn't sound like she lied so much as she didn't tell you everything," Andy said. He was eating one of his favorite things for lunch: a peanut butter and ketchup sandwich. It'd been so long since I'd eaten with him, I'd forgotten that he put ketchup on everything.

"A sin of omission rather than commission," Lark elaborated. All she was technically eating for lunch was an enormous apple. Except she kept stealing my potato chips.

"It's a sin all right." Corinne ignored Lark's advanced English and the fact she and I were committing or omitting the same sin and stole some of my chips too.

"Hey!" I complained. I'd forgotten what it was like eating with those guys. Most of my eating experiences involved shoveling in whatever was in front of me, not sharing it with girls who pretended to themselves they were on a diet.

"You've got to confront her, Gene," Corinne went on. "Tell her it's a sin that she lied to you and accuse her of stealing your skates."

"Wait a minute," I said. "I'm pretty sure she didn't steal my skates."

"You've got to make her feel guilty even if she didn't. She's the only one who can get them back for you." Corinne smiled a self-satisfied smile.

"No way," I took a big gulp of pop and burped.

"Gross!" said Lark.

"Sorry." I'd forgotten that I wasn't at the table of the apes with Brady.

"I'll go with you," Corinne offered.

"Like you and Sister Jude are on such good terms," I laughed. "I'll go by myself."

When we got up from lunch, Corinne and Andy walked in front of us with their arms around each other, which made me realize I didn't have the slightest idea what I was supposed to do with Lark. Lark wasn't helping. She just walked alongside of me, radiating awkward vibes, which were contagious.

"Uh, you know last night when I told you . . . you looked nice?" I asked Lark on the way to our locker.

"Yes?" She sounded interested in what I had to say which meant I must've been doing something right.

"I didn't mean it."

"Oh." Lark looked shocked and started walking faster like she was trying to get away from me.

"Wait." I ran to catch up with her as she reached our locker. "What I meant is you looked better than nice."

"Oh." She looked like she was going to cry.

I grabbed the book that she kept on the top shelf of the locker. I'd checked it out after she tried to hide it from me. It was her Dutch-to-English/English-to-Dutch dictionary. "I meant to say you look—uh—*schepsel*." I found the word for beautiful.

Lark looked puzzled.

"*Wildeman*," I added, figuring two words for beautiful were better than one.

She started laughing and tears ran down her face. "Gene, you just called me a beast."

"Oops." I looked again trying to get the right word. "*Schoon*? . . . beautiful." I said. And I didn't have to do anything more because she kissed me.

"You guys are disgusting." Brady elbowed his way into our locker and everything seemed like it was back to normal.

Making up with Lark or maybe I should be honest and say making out with Lark, gave me the confidence to confront Sister

Jude. I went over to the convent after school, walking around all of the spring puddles shimmering with car oil, wondering where in the hell I could find a dry place to skate anyway.

I took the stairs down to Sister Jude's office and found her hunched over her desk. I had to clear my throat and cough to get her attention. "Eugene," she said, "I've been meaning to call you."

Right. I'd stopped believing anything Sister Jude said.

"Sit down." She motioned me to a chair in front of her desk like she was the vice principal.

I stayed standing. "So Billy's your brother."

"You know my ministry with the homeless isn't really because of Billy. It's in spite of Billy." She rattled off this defense statement without looking at me. Then she sighed. "I do good work with everyone except Billy. He won't let me help him Eugene. I can't get it through his thick skull that I'm only trying to help him."

"Maybe someone else needs to help him." I sat down even though I hadn't planned on it. "My sister won't let me help her," I said. "Once I tried to teach her how to read and she grabbed the book and threw it at me."

Sister Jude finally looked at me. "I thought you might be able to help him. You do have a mutual enemy."

"Who—you?" I blurted out.

"Yes. You know, he told me that he thought you had a bad attitude toward me and he liked that."

"I don't really." I was embarrassed at how I used to laugh when Billy made fun of her.

"He wasn't that much older than you when he went to Vietnam." Her eyes clouded over like she was somewhere else. "He was so smart and talented. Maybe he would have had problems anyway, I don't know." She reached down and opened her deep bottom desk drawer. "Here honey, these are for you." She pulled out my skates, my long lost Shimas and dumped them on top of her desk. I just stared at them.

"How long have you had them?" I finally asked.

"I got them right after Schwartz talked to you. Schwartz tried to get Billy and the skates back but all he was able to do was take the skates."

"Isn't that a sin?" I thought back to my lunch conversation. "Stealing?"

"Retrieving stolen property?" She shrugged.

"It's not like you gave them back to me," I reminded her. "Schwartz even took me there when he knew Billy didn't have my skates."

"Please don't think too badly of me," Sister Jude said. She actually looked guilty instead of her usual superior self. "I was planning to give them to you eventually. I really thought you were the only one who could bring back Billy."

"Why didn't you just ask me to bring him back?" I asked.

"You would have done that?" she asked. "Without wanting to get something out of it for yourself?"

"Maybe." I shrugged. "Well, yeah." Why did she always assume I was such an asshole? Then I looked again at my skates which were grayer than I remembered, still tattooed with the cool black-and-blue soul signs.

I went to grab them but she was too fast and grabbed them first. "Here's your part of the speech." She shoved some papers in my outreached hand.

"Speech?" I'd forgotten about her plan for my public humiliation at the peace rally. I grimaced as I look at the typed pages which were filled with so many numbers they reminded me of my math book.

"Do you have a problem with it?" She tapped her hand on my skates like she was giving me a hint to the correct answer.

"No . . ." She glared at me and tightened her grip on my skates. "It just looks kind of boring."

"Boring?" She moved into self-righteous sermon mode. "Do you think it was boring for vets to live these statistics?"

Even though I was sure it was, I answered, "No, I guess I just need to spend some time reading it."

She loosened her grip on the skates and smiled. "*Schoon*," I said, grabbing them before she put them away.

"What?" She leaned over the desk like she wanted to grab them back.

I bent over and quick put them on. "*Schoon schepsel*," I said in my best Neanderthal voice as I stood up to check them out and flex my caveman biceps. "*Wildeman*," I added, thinking of her brother.

"Eugene, you can't have those on in here!"

"Sorry," I yelled back at her as I skated down the hall. I clomped up the stairs, then hit the puddled streets at full speed, splashing everywhere.

CHAPTER EIGHTEEN
PRACTICE

"We have to practice," Corinne said.

"Yeah," Andy agreed, even though he wasn't in the competition.

"Where?" I asked. "It's not like we can go to 3rd Lair." It had been snowing and raining on a daily basis. There was nowhere decent to skate except 3rd Lair, which was this awesome indoor skate park that cost money and was a freeway away.

"We've been going there." Andy shrugged like it was no big deal when he knew that I'd think it was a totally big deal.

"Where do you get the money and the ride?" I asked as it sank in that, while I'd been goofing around at the ice rink, they'd been really skating.

"My dad," Corinne said. "He's loaded, and he feels guilty for dumping me and my mom."

"Nice." I wondered just how loaded Corinne's dad was. Her mom obviously had no money at all. Maybe her dad just seemed rich by comparison.

"My mom's been driving us," Andy explained. "She thinks it's 'a good wholesome supervised activity' and I need more of that," he quoted.

My dad drove us there the next Saturday. My parents had decided to let me use my skates because Sister Jude had made such a big deal about how happy she was that I got them back. Now the message was that I was morally obligated to use them.

I invited Lark to come with us because I didn't want her to think I was ditching her, and I did better with an admiring audience. But she wasn't interested. "No way," she said. "I am too busy to be your little woman." She'd been doing all of this extracurricular stuff: French club (even though I made fun of her and said don't you speak Dutch?), the Green Tigers environmental club, a bit part in the spring musical, and debate (which she was especially good at). She was trying to pack years of experience into what was left of her school year. Since we'd gotten back together, Lark seemed different, more in power. I kind of liked her for that.

I was really out of practice. The only things I had going for me were my Shima 3's which felt so good. Like I'd lost a body part and it had magically regenerated.

"C'mon, Gene," Andy said. "Corinne's gonna whip your butt. You should see what she's capable of." Andy had his deck and was poised at the top of a half pipe. I dropped in and shot past him. I tried to channel Chris Edwards and catch some air. He got his nickname because of his amazing vert skating. He could fly thirteen feet over a half pipe.

"Can you do this?" Corinne took her turn on the ramp and flipped into a hand plant. With her helmet and bulky clothes no one knew she was a girl.

"Did you see that?" Some middle school kids stopped to watch but not for long. This was a working place. Everybody just kept at it even if they fell on their face all day. 3rd Lair was another concrete heaven: a big warehouse with nothing but ramps and pools, skating intensity and hip hop blaring.

It felt so good just to do skate tricks even when I wiped out. It was like my body'd been in a deep freeze and every time

I banged into something it started to thaw, which really hurt, but I was moving better by the second.

We took a break and got some Red Bull from the vending machine. For a while none of us said anything. We just stared at the video screen in the lounge with its endless loop of skate videos.

"Hey," Andy said. "It's our stuff."

"What?" Our stuff was safe at home on my computer.

"Those guys at Nollie Ollie. Check out the angle it's shot from—just like I suggested."

"Oh, yeah," I said. Then I remembered what came at the end of it: the bail section. "Let's go back and skate."

"Wait." Corrine pointed to a shot of me wiping out. "Hey, that's you, Snow."

"I don't always wipe out. I have videos of me at home doing a flat spin better than you could." It was true I only nailed it once out of fifty times but when I did, I did it better than anyone.

"I like it that they show you screwing up again and again," Corinne explained.

"I bet you do," I muttered.

"Because I can tell what you're doing wrong. I can help you."

"Oh," I said, torn between my need to look better and my need to be better.

"C'mon, let's go." She got up without waiting for an answer and spent the rest of the afternoon coaching me while Andy alternated between watching us, pretending to be interested and halfheartedly doing his own middle school tricks.

I felt bashed up and grateful when Andy's mom picked us up. I'd improved hugely in one day and I didn't have to pay for it.

"What does your dad do?" I asked Corinne on the way home.

"He's the vice president," she said.

"Of what?" "The United States?"

Andy laughed.

"I don't know, some company." She glared at me.

"What's your problem?" I asked. "All I did was ask about your dad."

"He's a Republican," Andy explained.

I laughed.

"Shut up," said Corinne.

"Boys, stop teasing Corinne," Andy's mom said. "Lots of people we know and love are Republicans and businessmen."

I did shut up at that. Most of my mom's family were Republicans and my dad was the only weirdo artist in his family.

"For example, Derrick Martin is Gene's best friend," Andy explained.

"Shut up," I said. "You're my best friend, you idiot."

Andy got this goofy dog smile on his face. "Yeah."

I skated every dry day I got and when I wasn't skating, I practiced driving. My sixteenth birthday was coming up and I'd told my parents all I wanted was to get my driver's license.

Dad had promised to take me for my test on my birthday. "What about a party?" Mom asked.

"I don't really need one," I told her. I didn't know how to explain I'd outgrown her pizza, pop, and movie parties. And who would I have invited other than Andy and the girls? Brady only went to parties to get drunk, and Sam would've made me feel embarrassed for asking and wouldn't have shown up.

"I'll invite Lark to go with us to Loaves and Fishes," Mom said.

"You scheduled us to work at Loaves and Fishes on my birthday?" I couldn't believe that even my do-gooder mother would do something that pathetic.

"I wasn't looking at a calendar. I just said we'd do the second Friday of the month. I'm sorry, Gene, we can do something nice to celebrate afterwards." She acted like I'd just awarded her worst mom of the year.

"It's okay," I assured her. "Invite Lark. She can tell her parents about it and freak them out."

"Loaves and Fishes would upset her parents?"

"They're very protective," I explained. "They think we live on a dairy farm."

"Oh, dear," Mom said.

"Time to go milk the cows," Dad announced.

Dad picked me up after school on the big day so we went directly to the driver's testing place which was way out in the suburbs. "You can drive if you want," he offered.

"No, thanks." I couldn't drive. I was too busy thinking about how to drive.

We had to wait in the car for the examiner guy. Wait and watch people come back from their tests. You could tell if they'd passed or not. They either jumped out of their cars and ran to hug the person who brought them there or they got out, stared at the ground and walked really slow like it was the fastest they'd ever move again.

The guy finally rapped on my window and Dad got out. "Good—" Dad started to say, but the guy interrupted him and started barking out orders. I thought my dad was going to wish me good luck, but it might as well have been good riddance.

The guy had me demonstrate that everything in our ancient Volvo was in working order. I started feeling paranoid that maybe he'd take points off because he didn't like our car. It seemed like most of the people who flunked drove beater cars.

Things seemed to go okay. I turned properly, even parallel parked and I thought I was passing although the guy didn't say anything. He only gave orders. Then he wrote stuff on his clipboard.

We drove around for what seemed like forever and I felt relieved. I'd done all the hard stuff and it had to be over soon. Then he yelled "STOP!" So I slammed on the brakes, even though the only stop sign I saw was a block away, and we both jerked back and just sat there. "Pull over," he ordered and I saw him write in big letters on the form attached to his clipboard: EMERGENCY STOP REQUIRED.

I followed his orders back to the parking lot. He handed me the form marked FAILED.

"I had to request an EMERGENCY STOP." He finally looked up from his clipboard.

"But . . ." I said, "I was slowing down. It was a block away."

"If I hadn't requested an EMERGENCY STOP, you wouldn't have stopped," he said like this was a fact. "You are a HAZARD."

"But . . ." I said, but he'd already moved on to flunk the next person.

Lark was there when I got home. She started to congratulate me but stopped as I walked in staring at the ground. All I wanted to do was to shut myself in my room and stare at the ceiling. Instead I had to go to Loaves and Fishes and celebrate my birthday when I wished I'd never been born. Well, that wasn't exactly true. I wished that evil driver's test guy had never been born. I wished I could retake the test and run him over. He could request emergency stops, he could plead for them but I wouldn't have listened. After all, I was a hazard.

When we tromped over to Loaves and Fishes, everyone was acting depressed out of respect for my failure. I felt the neighbors watching us as we headed towards St. Joan's. Because we supported Loaves and Fishes, they'd started giving us the evil eye just like we were bums ourselves.

Lily opened the door to the smell of fish. "Pee U!"

"Well, it is Lent," Mom told her.

"Loaves and Fishsticks," I said and everybody laughed except Lark.

"Fish on sticks?" She wrinkled her nose.

"What is lint?" Lily asked.

"The stuff you get between your toes from your socks," Dad explained with a straight face as we walked down the stairs and the fish ish smell got stronger. "Toe jam."

"Fish sticks, toe jam," Lark said. "This does not sound very appetizing."

We all laughed again while Mom explained American convenience food to Lark, Catholic food rules to Lily and my dad's weird sense of humor to everyone, including Dad.

The bums were impressed with Lark. Schwartz took me aside and said, "No offense but how did someone like you get a girl like her?"

"I don't know," I told him.

Sister Jude and Lark hit it off, of course. It turned out Lark was Catholic and because she knew more about the United States than the typical American teenager and wanted to know even more, she asked all the right questions. I kept waiting for Sister Jude to ask me how I got a girlfriend like Lark, but she didn't, which was probably the biggest compliment she had ever paid me.

For dessert, there was cake. A real birthday cake from a bakery. It had my name on it and actually tasted good. They didn't have any candles. Schwartz held up his lighter and I blew it out after everybody sang what must have been Happy Birthday, but sounded more like a funeral dirge.

"Did you buy this, Mom?" I asked, sneaking seconds because it was the first dessert I'd ever had at St. Joan's that wasn't petrified.

"No," she said. "I mentioned to Sister Jude that it was your birthday. If I had known, I would have brought candles."

"That's okay, Mom," I reassured her. "I kind of liked blowing out the lighter."

We left after I showed off my skills with the industrial dishwasher to Lark. "You are so macho with the heavy machinery," she said. Then she asked if she could try and we had the best time I'd ever had washing dishes.

I kind of said thank you to Sister Jude for the cake, because I knew it was a big deal for her to spend money on something as wasteful as a bakery cake with a personalized message.

She said something that wasn't like her at all about how I deserved it and how lucky they'd been to have me volunteer there. It made me feel like I should've done something more for her than pour coffee for the bums and play firefighter with the dishwasher. I really would have connected her with Billy without a reward. I wished she believed that.

When we got home, my mom brought out another cake.

"I'm going to go into a diabetic coma!" Lily complained.

"She's weird," I told Lark.

"She's cute," Lark disagreed. Lily smiled.

Nobody seemed to want to give me my birthday presents. I wondered why until I started opening them. They were all car-themed. First I opened the little box Lily gave me. It was a matchbox car. A Mustang convertible.

"Thanks," I said. "It's the car I've always wanted."

"Sorry you can't drive it," Lily said.

"Sure I can—vroooom." I rolled it on the floor and it went until it hit the leg of the dining room table.

"Gene!" Mom said.

"I hope it didn't hurt it. Nope, it's fine," I said, holding up the car and inspecting it.

"Eugene Snow, that's an antique table," Mom lectured but she didn't seem too worried.

"Yeah, it's just an old table," I agreed. "But this." I held the little car in the air like I'd won a prize. "This is a classic."

Lily giggled happily which made me feel good. I refused to let that driver's test asshole wreck my birthday.

Lark gave me a Bob Marley T-shirt, a skate magazine and my very own English-Dutch dictionary. "*Dunk.*" I thanked her.

Lark shook her head. "You mean *dank*. You are hopeless."

My parents gave me the usual boring good for you presents: clothes, books. Dad gave me some replacement parts for my skates which I really needed. "Thanks," I said, finding another little package in the pile.

"You'll use them eventually," Mom tried to reassure me, as I held up a set of keys on a miniature Mustang keychain.

"I'll use them tomorrow."

"Uh, Gene, you didn't pass. Remember?" Lily piped up while everyone else just looked at me.

Everyone in your life expects you to pass your driver's test so easily they plan your birthday presents around getting your license. But you don't pass because you get the driver's examiner from hell who, as far as you can tell, wouldn't pass his own mother. What do you do?

A. **Accept the fact that you are not over-the-road material and be grateful for the skate parts since this will be your permanent mode of transportation. As you get old, you might be the first person to skate with a walker but, heck, you could get a wheeled one.**

B. **Put all of your energy into plotting how to destroy the jerk, who not only destroyed your birthday, but destroyed the rest of your life. Something involving his face and tire treads.**

C. **Figure that the first test was just practice. Now that you know just how bad it can be you can take it again and drive like a little old grandma.**

"Duh!" I hit the side of my head for emphasis. "I'm going to try again tomorrow. One of you can take me, can't you?" Mom and Dad looked at me like they thought I was crazy.

Mom took me the next morning after we went around the neighborhood for a practice drive. "You don't have to start braking a block away from a stop sign," she said.

"Yes, I do," I told her. "If I get that guy again."

Instead of her usual *Little Engine* lecture, she started telling me passing wasn't everything and maybe I needed to give it more time. "Maybe we should go to a different exam station."

"No," I said. "Now I know what to expect."

When someone finally rapped on the car window, it was a different guy, dressed more casually than the first, in a Mister Rogers-style cardigan and tennis shoes. He smiled, then frowned as he read my paperwork.

"Good luck." Mom kissed me before she got out of the car, which was embarrassing but made the guy smile again.

When we got back home, I drove over to Andy's and sat in front of his house and honked. When he didn't come out, I called him on my cell. "Don't you hear me honking out front?"

Andy came running out pulling a pair of pants over his boxers. "Where's your mom or dad?" he asked.

"I dropped off my mom at home," I told him.

"But you flunked your test," he said, getting in the car anyway. "You can't drive by yourself."

"You're here," I said.

"Uh, Gene, I don't think I count. I'm not a licensed driver."

"Well, I am," I told him and drove around the neighborhood, slowing down every time I saw a stop sign in the distance.

Chapter Nineteen

Eugene

It annoyed me that everyone at school not only knew I got my license, they also knew I flunked the first time. I was almost glad there was the peace rally to take everyone's mind off my driving history. Even if I did have to give this lame speech with Sister Jude.

The plan was the entire school would walk out in protest and go to the peace rally if the U.S. went to war with Iraq. Well, almost the entire school. Derrick Martin told everyone he wouldn't go and hoped we all got in trouble for unexcused absences.

But the day of the walkout, Derrick did go. He elbowed me in the hall. "I'm going to a counter rally, dude. We're going to out-yell you lame peaceniks."

Sam and Brady were on the basketball court. "Basketball for peace!" Brady yelled and Sam flashed us a peace sign as I went by with the girls and Andy.

We took the bus to the first part at the U, then had to take it downtown, which was kind of annoying since Corinne kept saying, "Couldn't you have gotten your parents' car, Snow?"

"No," I told her for the hundredth time. "Give me a break. I have to do this speech and I need to concentrate." I was studying Sister Jude's speech about vets and their problems. It figured that she was going to say the inspirational stuff and had assigned me the stuff no one would listen to.

My parents were so excited I was doing this. My mom kept telling everyone that Sister Jude said this was practice for my career in public service. Both of them had to work but they were having some friend of theirs videotape it. I guess they'd add it to their collection of my most embarrassing moments, along with potty training and wiping out on my bike the first time without training wheels.

"At least you get an excused absence from school." Andy was wearing his "MAKE LOVE NOT WAR" shirt. "Your parents are the biggest peaceniks around. They'd probably ask that you be excused even if you weren't giving a speech. Maybe we could get them to call in and ask that the whole school be excused."

"Do you think they'd call in for me?" Lark was trying hard not to worry about having an unexcused absence. I'd talked her into going to this rally so she didn't get the wrong idea about Americans. People had started asking her if she was French, implying that she was anti-American because of her European accent. It was as weird as people calling french fries freedom fries because France wasn't supporting us going to war. Lark was going back to Belgium at the end of the school year and I couldn't stand the thought of some of the things she could tell people.

"Our stop," I said and most of the bus which was full of high school kids got off.

As we walked with the crowd, I wished I had my skates. This was so much better than that old people's peace march. Maybe it was good this was on a weekday when peace drones like my parents had to work. Andy started singing "War (What Is It Good For?)" which was a major improvement over that whiney "Give Peace A Chance."

Through all the noise, I heard Corinne's phone ring. She answered it and was just walking along talking when some guy started harassing her. "You spoiled rich kids with your cell phones," he yelled. "Go back to school!"

Corinne stopped in mid-sentence and started pushing her way through the crowd toward the guy. "Wait." I followed her. "He's a vet." I recognized some of the guys he was with from Loaves and Fishes.

"So? As far as I'm concerned, he can go back to his war." She said this loud enough for him and the little army of vets who surrounded him to hear.

I hurried behind her, then I noticed who was standing beside this guy. "Billy!" I said.

"I brought him." Schwartz, who was standing on Billy's other side, shoved him at me like he was making a delivery.

"I don't have your skates," he said, his face twitching. I expected him to take off but he just stood there, like he'd been waiting for me.

"It's okay. I found them."

"After you almost beat him up," Corinne said, forgetting about the guy she wanted to beat up.

"C'mere, Billy." I got an idea. "I want to show you something."

He seemed pretty nervous, but I took the chance that if I just started walking, he'd follow me. I headed to the stage where the speakers were supposed to wait.

"Hey," Billy said. He spotted Sister Jude and started to turn away.

"Wait, Billy," I said. "You knew she'd be here. You knew she'd be speaking. You've got to see her sometime."

"She tortures me," Billy whined.

"Yeah, I know." I looked calmly into his panicked eyes. "But when you're not around, she tortures me and I can't take it anymore. I already have to deal with my own sister."

But he wasn't listening to me. He'd already gone up to her. "Hey, Judy," he said.

"Billy!" She got this big smile on her face and hugged him while he just stood there like a statue.

"Godammit, Judy. You torture me. See?" He turned to me.

"Eugene?" I shrugged modestly, waiting for her to get down on her knees and thank me. "Eugene, I can't go on stage now, I'll lose him."

"Bring him with us," I suggested. We didn't get much time to argue. We were scheduled to go first and had to head up there.

Sister Jude took the microphone and started to say something but stopped as Billy twisted out from under her arm and walked away. "Billy—wait!" she said. "You can't do this to me." She turned and followed him off the stage, leaving me standing there wanting to say the same thing.

"Uh . . ." I stepped up to the mic, then stood there for a minute, listening to the PA system amplify my uncertainty. There were a lot of people there and they were finally quieting down, waiting for me to say something.

"Talk into the mic. We can't hear you," someone heckled.

I could hear Derrick's group from across the street chanting. I couldn't let Derrick take over, so I tried again. "Ummm, my name is Gene Snow." I backed up as the sound system squawked. I looked down at my page of statistics. Good for Sister Jude that she got Billy back but what what I supposed to do? I thought of Paul Wellstone and how he said stuff from his heart. I crumpled the statistics into a ball.

"Go U-Gene!" It sounded like Schwartz.

"Yeah," I said. "My name is really Eugene, which is kind of a ummm . . ." I stopped there to think of an appropriate adult expression. "Nerd name," I continued. Some of the kids from my school started laughing. "But I'm actually pretty proud of it," I said, realizing as I said it that in a weird way, this was true. "My parents named me after Eugene McCarthy who was this guy who ran for president and was against the Vietnam War." At this point, some people started clapping and whistling. "I work as a volunteer with Vietnam vets at St. Joan's. A lot of people complain because they don't want them in our neighborhood."

"Uptight yuppie scum!" This time I was sure it was Schwartz and for once I was grateful for his big mouth.

"Um, Sister Jude, who runs the program, was supposed to talk now, but she needs to be with her brother who's a vet. He's kind of a friend of mine, even though he has a pretty confusing life so he doesn't trust me or anybody very much. Anyway, his life kind of sucks and I think it doesn't help that something bad happened to him in Vietnam and now nobody wants him in their neighborhood." I looked around and got the creeps when I realized everyone seemed to be listening to me.

"Anyway," I said, "I get these lectures at school about how I'm supposed to learn from my mistakes and everybody always says the Vietnam War was a big mistake so why are we doing it again?" People clapped at this, which made me feel brave. "Paul Wellstone . . ." Someone whistled when I said his name which made me feel even braver. "Paul Wellstone told me and my parents that he couldn't justify sending kids to this war. He did the right thing, and we need to umm do the right thing too." People started to clap and hoot at this and I looked back nervously at the emcee who saved my butt by putting his arm around me and leading me away from the microphone.

I walked back into the crowd and heard people murmuring around me. "Gene, I am so proud of you." Lark hugged me.

"You seemed pretty nervous," Corinne said. "Maybe you should have introduced yourself as Rodeo Snow."

"No way!" Andy, who had never disagreed with Corinne once during his months as president of the Corinne Camden fan club shook his head. She made a face at him. "Everything you said was just right," he said. And because he said it, I decided it was true.

CHAPTER TWENTY

BEST FRIENDS

Andy and I were definitely back to being best friends. We even had a baby together. In Ms. Mansfield's psychology class, we had to take care of a sack of flour with a partner as a form of academic birth control. Andy and I really got into it. We wrapped our flour baby with duct tape, drew an evil looking face on him and covered him with skull tattoos using a black sharpie.

My mom came up with an old baby carrier: a sling to carry him in front of you so you could keep your hands free. "Can't we just throw him in our backpacks?" I complained.

"Would you throw a baby in a backpack?" she asked.

Andy raised his caterpillar eyebrows and shrugged. Of course we would.

"This little dude is heavy," Andy complained as he picked him up. "We should have gotten a five-pound bag and told Ms. Mansfield he was premature."

"Poor little Oops," I said.

"Oops?" Mom questioned. "Why in the world would you name him Oops?"

"Two reasons, Mrs. S." Andy tossed Oops to me and a little cloud of flour flew out around him as he hit my hands. "One, because his existence is a mistake. Teenage pregnancy—Oops!"

"That's terrible!"

"And . . ." Andy pretended to fumble and almost dropped him when I tossed him back. "Because we can't really be trusted to take good care of him. Oops!" He threw him high in the air, then barely bothered to catch him.

"I hope you boys are taking this assignment seriously," Mom lectured.

"We are," I assured her. "We're learning the lesson that teenage boys shouldn't have babies." I put him down on the floor and used him as a foot rest.

"He's ugly," Lily pointed out. "What's he supposed to be—a pirate?"

"Shh, you'll hurt his feelings," I told her.

"He's a goth baby," Andy said. He picked him up and pretended to burp him, letting out a humongous belch.

"Gross!" Lily shrieked and ran out of the room while Mom shook her head at us.

Not only did I have Andy back as my disgustingly funny best friend, but Corinne had become my skate partner again. We spent all our free time practicing for the street comp. Lark and Andy didn't seem to mind because they knew how important it was. Corinne was so good. Every time I thought I was good at something, she did it just as good or better.

The night before the competition, I drove us to Nollie Ollie. Rumor had it that it would be a comp stop. "I can't wait until I get my license," Corinne said. "My dad's gonna buy me a car." I couldn't imagine my parents buying me a car. It was a big deal they were letting me use my skates again.

I started messing around, skating more into each move than I had to. I caught Corinne looking at me kind of how I looked at her when I thought no one was watching. "What?" I stopped. "Am I doing something wrong?"

"No." She seemed embarrassed instead of her usual bossy self. "It's weird." She looked thoughtful. "I skate like an athlete but you skate like an artist."

"Oh. So I like skate gay?" I blurted out.

"No." She turned red. "I just like the way you move." Now I was turning red. She returned to her usual bossiness. "I'll show you. This is how I grind." She skated fast and hard and did her typical clean tough move. "This is how you do it." She started out with long strides and tried to do the same thing in slow motion like she was a ballet dancer but wiped out.

"I'm not that bad."

"Well, if I could skate like you I would," Corinne said.

"If I could skate like you I would," I said. We stood staring at each other for a second.

"Watch." I skated away as fluidly as possible then jumped the concrete ledge like I was doing a hip hop move.

Corinne scrambled over, grinning. "Yeah. How'd you do that?"

"Lengthen your stride," I said. "No, like this." I grabbed her around the waist and positioned her legs so she was almost doing the splits.

She laughed. "You have got to be kidding."

"No, really. Like this." I got behind her and pushed one leg out at a time with my legs from behind.

She turned toward me and was so close I could see the metal holding the stone on her nose ring. "Snow, you are so full of shit," she said and didn't move.

You finally get the chance to let the girl you can't stop thinking about know how you're thinking about her and, of course, the chance has to come right before this big

competition when the last thing either of you need is the distraction of a complicated love life but it feels like you might never get this chance again. What do you do?

A. Tell her, "Look, I know that your boyfriend is my best friend and my girlfriend is your best friend, but even though that should stop me from thinking about you it just makes me think about you even more, so I figured I might as well tell you."

B. Keep your mouth shut and and know that when you're ninety years old, alone and miserable, you'll have to wonder if your life would have been different if you had told her.

C. Well, you don't get to C because she kisses you.

She kissed me, then skated away and started working on stuff like it had never happened.

CHAPTER TWENTY-ONE
RODEO SNOW

"Rodeo Snow," I told the guy at the registration table.

"Nice name." He looked up from his computer printout and handed me a business card. "Octane. Marketing," he said, like his name didn't matter.

Octane was this new skate company sponsoring the competition. They were offering a prize of 500 dollars, free skates, and the chance to be on some demos. The marketing guy was wearing a GET PUMPED/OCTANE T-shirt under an expensive-looking black leather jacket.

I hung around to hear what he said to Corinne, but he didn't say anything, didn't give her a card, didn't even look at her. I glanced at the card, then started to jam it in my pocket.

But Corinne grabbed it and inspected it. "Don't you get it?" She looked disgusted. "That marketing guy from Octane likes your name. You could win this."

"You're really good." I grabbed it back. "You could win this."

The streets swarmed with skaters. We were by the lakes and our arch enemy school, Southwest. It was the rich kids' part of town. We river rats didn't usually hang out there. But that day every skater in the Twin Cities showed up. There were all sorts of skate start ups selling their wares: T-shirts, skate parts, DVDs. The air vibrated with hip hop and adrenaline, the click clack of skates everywhere.

"Check that out." I pointed out a rail surrounding the school, high on a concrete ledge, that a bunch of losers were trying—and failing—to grind.

"We can do better than that." I jumped up and skated it easily. Then I watched Corinne grind part way, do her signature twist and slide the rest of it backwards. She was in total competitive mode. It was like last night had never happened. Fine. I could be just as competitive as she was. And once I won, she'd have to admit that it was me she liked, not Andy.

We went all over the Cities. Brady, who just got his license, drove. We were crammed into his rust-bucket car—all my old friends and Lark and Corinne.

"Can we double buckle?" Lark asked, squishing in on my lap.

"No seat belts." Brady gunned it.

"It's your turn to win, Gene," Sam said.

Corinne glared at me. I couldn't see Andy but I knew she was mad at him too. After all what did Sam know? We were the ones who'd seen her skate.

Our first stop was the Green Giant: this green rail of death in a southern suburb. It descended this hill behind a school. It wasn't very steep but it was ungodly long.

There were so many of us I didn't know how they were going to eliminate enough people, how anybody was going to stand out among all the wannabes. I lost track of Corinne. They'd divided us into three heats. The best in each competed for the final prize. At least I wasn't directly competing against Corinne. I wasn't sure I wanted to compete against anybody. A lot of guys there were probably as good as me.

"The Jolly Green Giant!" Andy announced as we got out of the car. "Ho, ho, ho." Leave it to Andy to make something intimidating sound like a dumb commercial. I watched a couple of guys ahead of me navigate the rail a short ways then wipe out. Then it was my turn. I stood at the top, remembering how Corinne did it, took a deep breath, jumped up and on and hit this great beautiful glide like I was exhaling down the rail, my breath moving my body.

I hit the end and spectacularly slammed into the muddy ground. Maybe I could stand out. It sounded like it from the whoops around me. "Go, Rodeo," my friends yelled.

We had to stay until Corinne went which gave me plenty of time to see some of my feared competitors eliminated. I started to feel cocky. What was their problem that they couldn't make it down this basic rail? Then it was Corinne's turn, and I lost my confidence. So I did it beautifully, so what? So I was just a pretty boy. She, as usual, put her own mark on something straightforward. She turned and twisted and did this amazing hop at the end. She was crazy but always in control. It made you want to watch her do anything just to see what she'd do next.

"Hey, you got some competition there, Gene," Sam said as we packed into the car again.

"Yeah." I decided I could at least acknowledge that much to Corinne.

They started going on about Paul—the guy who won last year. "He's technically so good," Sam said.

"What about Corinne?" Lark asked.

"Yeah," said Andy.

"Sorry." Sam shrugged. "Guess I missed you, Corinne."

"Attention deficit," explained Brady.

"Well, she was amazing," I said. "Your loss."

"You losers." Now Corinne was pissed at the right people.

The next couple of sites were okay. Nothing as interesting or dramatic as the Green Giant: suburban staircases and handrails. The car ride was getting weirder though.

"You got my attention," Brady told Corinne.

"I had no idea you were so good." Sam actually sounded sincere. He turned to me. "You've really got some competition."

Corinne smiled at me, looking pretty satisfied with herself.

"Shut up," I said, wishing I'd taken my own vehicle.

I was itching to get back into the city so I was glad when our next stop was Hidden Falls, this big deserted park butted up against the river in St. Paul. People piled out of their cars and skaters started climbing up the picnic shelter. It was this collection of seven or eight connecting rooms open to the outside, each with a sloping yellowish roof. Looking out over it was like looking over stucco sand dunes. It was like a series of halfpipes suspended in the air. I had to channel my inner Airman.

"I'm glad I don't have to do that," Andy said from below. "I'm afraid of heights."

When it was my turn, I hopped from the edge and rock and rolled it. Up, leap, down. Again and again, weaving across the rooftops. I was just getting into it when my time was up.

I had to watch all of these lame people who hardly took advantage of this great skate until Corinne finally went. All those hours at 3rd Lair had paid off. She rode the roofs like a halfpipe roller coaster. I really wanted to try it again. Just watching her I knew how I'd really want to do it. But just as she slowed down, someone yelled, "The cops are here!"

Everyone scattered but I just stood there watching Corinne. She skated to an open space between the roofs, flew high, then stuck it and scrambled down. I forced myself to follow her as my friends yelled for me. Brady kicked mud on his license plate before he jumped in and peeled off past the cops and their notepads.

"I didn't get enough time there," I complained.

"You have to use the time you get." Corinne shrugged.

That sucked. I knew I could be as good as she was. I had to use every chance I got to my advantage. No more waiting for just the right situation.

We headed to Minneapolis and left the St. Paul cops behind, stopping at the low yellow rails at the Farmer's Market. These were deceptively boring to someone who was a skate park weenie. But not me. I was a street skater, and I got to strut my stuff. Now I was determined to use everything. I danced the rails. It was like if you got to skate the balance beam in gym class: hip hop heaven. Corinne went for an extremely rapid wicked ride: backwards. I felt sorry for anyone who had to go after us. They were basically doing a gym routine.

We moved on to Loring Park in downtown Minneapolis. There were tons of places to skate there. It was a skater's paradise. Finally they narrowed it down. There were just three skaters left, one from each heat: me, Corinne, and the winner from last year, the old school guy named Paul. We got the luxury there of choosing where we wanted to skate.

Paul headed for the Dandelion Fountain and skated the granite tiers. It made me think of *Dare to Air*, Chris Edward's video, the first inline video ever made. In *Dare to Air*, they skated a fountain that was on. It was such a rush to watch them skate through the spray. It was too early in the season for the water to be on that day. Paul's trick was dry anyway.

Corinne headed over to the horseshoe pits. She started in the middle and jumped the two-foot-high wood barriers that stood there in rows. The trick was that to clear them she had to take them diagonally. Everyone went crazy as she pulled it off. Even the old guys who were waiting to play their game of horseshoes. "That's my bionic babe," bragged Andy.

Then it was my turn. This was where my winter spent studying the Dre Powell DVD came in. The one where he did the most beautiful cess slide in existence. I called it the Jesus slide. It was like he was skating on water. I skated the stage, rushing up the funky asphalt ramp, taking off at the block of concrete. I landed in a hockey stop onstage and skimmed over the concrete like it was water, not disturbing the surface.

Beautiful. Dre Powell, Jesus walk on water beautiful. My body felt like it was made of air and water. It was a floating, fluid thing. Someone wolf whistled. I caught Corinne's eye. She took her hair out of its ponytail, tossing it over her shoulder as she turned away. She was pissed. She hated it when I skated prettier than her.

I could barely stand to be in the car on the way to the last heat. "Nice job back there," I told Corinne. She ignored me. My friends wouldn't shut up with their play by play analysis. Even Lark was annoying me. "I'm so nervous for you two." She squeezed my hand like she was squeezing her nervousness into me. I listened as Sam gave us advice on what we should do next. Then I listened to Brady say the exact opposite. I looked at Corinne. She wasn't listening. She'd gone to some place inside herself: the place where she could win. I took my hand from Lark's and plugged my ears. I wanted to go there too but I couldn't concentrate.

The final heat was where we anticipated. The place I knew best: Nollie Ollie. We drew straws to determine the order. It was Paul, then Corinne, then me. Paul was good but really old school. He did everything rock solid but with no personality. It was really down to just Corinne and me. And we were at Nollie

Ollie, the place where I'd perfected my blindside halfcab soul. The place where she'd kissed me.

Paul cleared the stairs—nothing special. But being proficient kept him in the comp. He'd get a second turn after Corinne and I were done and he could blow us away the next time.

Corinne brushed past me to go next. I'd seen her fly down these stairs hundreds of times. I'd seen her push herself to do harder and harder tricks and wipe out too. I held my breath and watched as she geared up to go. I shouldn't have been watching. I should've been focusing on myself. But I couldn't help it. What would she do? Would she play it safe which would still be better than Paul or would she risk blowing it?

She skated hard toward the stairs, took off and spinned. Everyone held their breath. It was the most incredible skating I'd ever seen. I had no idea what her trick was even called. It was like we were witnessing something none of us had ever seen before. It was like she was a projectile hurtling through the air towards its target. She knew exactly where and how she was going to land and nailed it. Everyone went crazy as she skated off.

I stood there stunned, forgetting, at first, that it was my turn. Then I thought why bother when she'd already won. No one could say she wasn't the best skater there. I couldn't do that trick if I'd practiced for a million years.

I took a deep breath and skated towards the stairs. I could feel everyone's expectations like they thought it might be possible to do better than that. "Go, Rodeo!" Lark yelled. I turned and saw her standing up front with my family who must have come for the end. I went on, trying to forget my mom's worried face. Shit! My left wheels caught in a crack and I felt myself lurch forward and fall. I pushed myself up with one hand as the crowd collectively groaned. I glanced over at the judges who nodded for me to continue. So I circled around and headed out again avoiding the gouge in the concrete. I skated like a bat out of H-E-double hockey sticks and whizzed through the air. It was the best tweaked flat spin I'd ever done, but it wasn't good enough. People clapped and hooted but nothing like they did for Corinne. We all wanted to see her do her trick again.

Paul went for a last time, carefully avoiding the crack which I could see from the sidelines was a lethal pothole. People clapped like they were giving him encouragement.

Then it was Corinne again. She headed towards the stairs and I could tell she was in that other place: the winning place. Watch out for the crack, I wanted to say as she skated toward it. She was so focused, of course she'd see it. But she didn't. She tripped forward, wiped out. But she was up in a split second, pushing off the ground with both hands, ready to try again.

The Octane guy was whispering something to the judges. "Wait," one of them said. "You've forfeited your turn by falling."

"But . . ." she said.

"It was a completed fall, " the judge said and motioned me forward.

You've just been asked to help cheat the best skater in the Twin Cities out of their rightful title. Everyone is waiting: the judges, Corinne, the grumbling crowd. What do you do?

A. Say "No way." Refuse to go until they let her skate.
B. Wait for Corinne to, as usual, stick up for herself.
C. Fall too—now what will they do?
D. Skate your turn since everyone's waiting.

"Hey asshole, stop wasting our time," someone yelled. Then everybody got really worked up and noisy.

"But . . ." I started to say and turned to Corinne. She didn't say anything. She just stood there white-faced and silent like she was in shock. I started to go over to the judges' table, but the Octane guy shook his head and waved me away like nobody was going to budge on this and all I was doing was prolonging the agony.

So I went. I skated and I didn't fall. I skated towards the ledge and did a decent blindside halfcab sole which I owed to Corinne. Some people clapped, I thought. I wasn't sure. I couldn't really take it in.

One of the judges motioned Corinne, Paul, and me to the top of the stairs. The Octane guy stopped, talked to the judges and then stood beside us. "We have a winner," he announced to the crowd, then paused for effect: "Rodeo Snow!" he shouted, grabbing my arm and pulling it up in the air. At first no one said anything. Then people started booing and complaining. The Octane guy and his staff start chanting "Ro-de-o, R-o-de-o" but hardly anyone joined in.

I looked to Corinne. Why wasn't she sticking up for herself like she usually did? Didn't she know I depended on her and her big mouth to tell people what was screwed up about a situation? Paul looked at me like I should say something.

The Octane man handed me a check, grabbed my arm again and waved it over my head. "Thanks," I told him, even though I should've said, "No thanks, I didn't win." I should've turned to Corinne and said, "She did." How in the heck was I supposed to do that without dying of embarrassment? I knew Paul Wellstone would have said I should do what I thought was right but that was easy for him, he had lots of experience. I thought I knew what was right, but I didn't know how I was supposed to do it.

The Octane guy gave me a demo schedule and another business card as Paul and Corinne headed down to the crowd. I could hardly pay attention.

"Give me a call." He looked smug like he'd won me instead of me winning the comp. He slapped me on the back.

"Rodeo Snow," he said. "Nice name."

CHAPTER TWENTY-TWO

OOPS!

"I get it," Mom said on the ride home. "I finally get how you do it. You're not afraid of falling, are you?"

"No, I guess not." I was distracted by the sight of Andy and Corinne as we left, sitting on the top of the steps, in their own world.

"I think you develop that fear as you get older." She just went on and on. She was so excited I'd both won and not seriously injured myself she was oblivious to how under-enthused I was.

"I'm sorry, Gene." Lark squeezed my hand. I felt a twinge of guilt. Lark would have never dumped me again. I was a jerk to have even thought about dumping her.

"Gene cheated," Lily announced from the back seat.

"I didn't cheat."

"How did you win then? Corinne was better than you."

"Lily, that's not very nice," Mom said.

"It's true," I said.

"Gene, give yourself credit for your incredible recovery," Dad said as he pulled into our alley. My parents were the only people in the whole crowd who thought I had legitimately won. But they always thought I was the best even when I was bad at something. Parents.

"You picked yourself up after you fell and did really well the next time," Mom pointed out.

"That's because they let me. They wouldn't let Corinne."

"But she fell more than you—on both hands," Dad said.

"So?"

"Wasn't that the rule?" Mom, the queen of rules asked.

"Yeah, the rule they just made up," I said. "She should've won but they wouldn't let her."

"Probably because she's a girl," Lily added. Lark nodded in agreement.

As soon as Lark left, I called Corinne. "I need to talk to you."

"Why? Want to rub it in?"

"No," I said. "I just need to talk to you."

"A bunch of us are going to the river tonight," she said. "I'll leave early and call you so we can meet there."

"Okay." I wondered why I hadn't heard about this before. Wouldn't everybody want me there? I had won after all. I waited for Andy or Brady or even Sam to call, but I didn't hear from anyone but Corinne.

I walked to the park bench, under the street lights, where I had sat so long ago at the end of last summer with Corinne. The air smelled too sweet like everything had gone overboard with blossoming. Corinne finally walked up. It was weird meeting without our skates. They'd been our way of belonging together. Her fists were clenched in the pockets of her hoodie. Her face was pale and unhappy, framed by her hood. She sat down and turned to me, the red stone where her nose was pierced catching the light like a drop of blood.

"So?" She stared at me.

"I didn't ask to win."

"You mean you beat me without even trying?" She yanked her hood off and her hair escaped, messy and angry.

"No. I tried really hard to beat you but I couldn't."

"But you did." Her voice was mean. "You won. Or didn't you understand that's what it meant when they gave you that check and everyone was yelling your name."

"Everyone wasn't yelling my name. It was just the Octane assholes yelling for Rodeo Snow. I only won because that Octane guy wants someone named Rodeo Snow to promote his stuff. I don't want to win that way."

"What's the matter with you? You're such a noble Boy Scout. If I had won I wouldn't't've cared how. All I wanted to do was win."

All I wanted to do was win her, I realized. "Why did you kiss me?" I blurted out because that's what I really wanted to know.

She snorted at me in disgust and for a second I was afraid she wasn't going to answer. "I kissed you because I couldn't stand it any longer," she said. "I was sick of you wanting to kiss me and not doing anything about it."

"Like what was I supposed to do? Andy's my best friend."

"You don't know how winning works," she said. "If you want something you go for it no matter what." I just stared at her. " You don't even know me," she complained. "You think I'm this inner city skater. Well, I come from Barrington which is this rich suburb. Not Chicago. And my dad's a Republican and I think I am too. I am so tired of hanging out with losers like you. You even act like a loser when you win."

She looked at me like she was going to say something terrible and then she did: "I broke up with Andy. I'm tired of being someone's girlfriend. I'm tired of being treated like a girl."

"Oh." Somehow I felt responsible. "I'm calling Octane and returning my check," I told her.

"Suit yourself."

We sat for a few more minutes not saying anything. Usually the presence of Corinne had this effect on me of blocking out all thoughts of Lark, but instead I kept hoping someone had asked Lark to come that night. All I wanted to do right then was to hang out with her.

A car coasted up and stopped. It was Brady. He was probably out of gas and trying to get by on fumes. Everybody piled out. My entire history of friends: Brady, Andy, Sam, then Lark. Brady had brought his Neanderthal influence, a bottle of Jagermeister, which he passed to Andy. Andy adjusted Oops who hung at his stomach from his baby sling. He took an angry swig as he walked towards us. "Have a drink, Rodeo." He held out the bottle.

"Uh, no thanks." I stuffed my hands in my pockets. Lark looked at me nervously and mouthed, "Get me out of here." I wished I could figure out how.

"What's the matter, Rodeo? We're all drinking to you. Can't you drink to yourself?" Andy took a drunken chug before returning the bottle to Brady. We headed down to the river to the beach where Brady, the pyromaniac, started a campfire.

"So what are you going to do with your check, Rodeo?" Andy asked, pushing between me and Lark.

"Probably give it to the poor," said Sam.

"Shut up," I said, pushing the bottle away as Andy pushed it at me again. This was not the victory celebration I had imagined.

"What's with that sack of flour? You take it everywhere," Sam asked Andy.

"My mom makes me." Andy sounded sheepish. "Besides I like him."

"I'll take him," I offered. Andy was in such bad shape I could see him squeezing Oops to death and lowering our grade.

"Like I'd trust you, Romeo," Andy said pointedly.

I didn't know if he realized what he'd just said. I looked at Corinne but she was finishing off Brady's bottle. Lark's face was in darkness.

"Let's go down to the railroad bridge." Brady had just gotten the fire going, but his attention deficit was kicking in.

"Yeah," Corinne agreed.

We scrambled down the path toward the bridge, this rectangle of rusted crisscrossed metal suspended high over the river. "Time to climb," yelled Brady, running ahead, then pulling himself up the concrete footing. We all followed. I offered a hand to Lark once I was up and then didn't let go. The light from the streetlight lit up her face and she smiled her candy-red smile at me.

"Who's going out to the middle?" Brady asked. Not me. Brady had this tendency to get other people in trouble for his viewing enjoyment.

"C'mon, Rodeo!" Andy started walking on the planks laid out halfway over the metal girders.

"No way." Lark squeezed my hand. "Don't do it."

"I'll go." Corinne started out after Andy, but then stopped once she reached the end of the boards and had to consider jumping to the metal siderails.

"What's the matter, Rodeo? Can't even go as far as a girl?" Andy taunted. He was really out there.

Your best friend's drunk, hanging over the Mississippi like a sheet to dry. There's a slight chance that, if you do the absolute perfect right thing you can save him and an enormous chance that if you do the wrong thing or even got it right, but made one tiny microscopic mistake, both of you will die. What do you do?

A. Nothing and hope that Corinne, whose fault this all is, will come to her senses and get her butt back out there.

B. Start inching out, telling yourself not to look down, telling yourself you're not taking one giant step toward your death, you're taking baby steps toward your best friend.

C. Jump, plunge to your cold wet death and get it over with.

"Stay there, Andy," I yelled. "I'm coming to get you." "Always do what you think is right," I could hear Paul Wellstone tell me. "Even if it gets you in trouble." He should have said even though it always gets you in trouble.

"I'm waiting," Andy yelled. He sat in the space at the bottom of a metal x and started messing with Oops in his baby sling. I tried to focus on inching out to him safely and, at the same time, watched to make sure he didn't do anything stupid.

"Hey, Rodeo." Andy tossed Oops in the air and almost lost his balance as he caught him. He held Oops out leaning over the emptiness between the bridge and the river. "Hey, Rodeo, you have a responsibility to the ones you love."

"Andy, stop it—it's not funny," Corinne yelled.

"I guess that depends on who you love, doesn't it?" he yelled back. He turned to me. "Catch." He threw Oops towards me and I dodged, clinging to the cold metal to keep from falling. I held my breath as Oops hurtled past and its silvery bulk hit the water.

"Shit, why didn't you catch him?" Andy said, as I finally got close to him. "You let me down." We sat there watching the glint of light that must have been Oops disappear down the dark ribbon of river.

"I'm sorry." I put one arm around him and braced myself with the other.

"I really liked him," Andy said. "Didn't you like him?"

"He was just a sack of flour. Let's go back, okay?"

We inched our way back. I talked Andy through it, nonstop. It was like my words were weaving a net under us.

"Just follow my directions," I told him. "Remember my mom always says if you follow directions you can do anything." Andy put his feet and his hands where I told him with exaggerated oversized movements. There was no sound except for the static of traffic and the sound of my voice. I imagined our friends on the riverbank, not wanting to watch but watching.

When we finally reached the place where we could climb down, I heard Lark say, "Thank God."

And Corinne repeated, "Andy, that wasn't funny."

Andy, who had been in this trance, hypnotized by my voice, woke up. "Oops!" He pretended to fall. The guys laughed. I couldn't believe they thought that was funny. Andy laughed too. He sounded relieved, then all of the sudden he stopped, scrambled to keep his footing. Brady and Sam kept laughing.

Corinne yelled, "Andy!" I grabbed him, trying to pull him back, but his flailing weight pulled us off balance and we fell. We tumbled down the slope like we were nothing but a couple of sacks of flour and no one could do anything but watch us.

Chapter Twenty-Three

Airman

Even though you would've thought he'd be grateful because I saved his life twice: first getting him almost off the bridge and second slowing his fall down the riverbank, Andy wasn't speaking to me. Not only was he blaming me for Corinne, he thought I was responsible for his being grounded, maybe for the rest of his life. This was my fault. Brady dropped us at Andy's house after we crawled up the riverbank and limped to the car. By the time I walked Andy in, I was too tired to do anything but tell the truth to his parents while Andy threw up in the bathroom.

What he didn't know is I didn't exactly have it easy. My mom, who had been so excited about me not being afraid to fall, treated me like I needed to wear a helmet to go to the bathroom.

Corinne wasn't speaking to me either. But then, I wasn't sure she was speaking to anyone. Amazingly, Lark didn't hate me. It wasn't like I told her I'd been thinking of dumping her for Corinne, but we both knew that the fact she was leaving at end of the school year had changed things. I was smart enough to realize I needed to tell her this part of the truth over and over again: how lucky I was to have her right then.

"I'm going to call that Octane guy and give up my title," I told Lark. "I'm going to tell him to give it to Corinne."

"Wow," Lark said. "You're my hero."

"I've been too much of an asshole to be a hero," I said.

"Heroes are just ordinary people trying not to be assholes," Lark told me.

I waited until no one was around to listen to my awkwardness, then started pacing back and forth across the house as I called the Octane guy. Amazingly, he answered, although he sounded irritated and didn't take me seriously. "C'mon," he said. "We've got a whole ad campaign we're developing around you, around that name."

"I'm sending back the check," I told him. "I can give you Corinne's phone number."

"Who?"

"Corinne. The person who really won."

"Corinne," he repeated. "Oh, that girl." He laughed. "She's not really our demographic." He laughed again. "Keep the check. Just think about it."

I kept the check even though I didn't cash it. I didn't know how to get it to him anyway. There were tons of things I could spend it on: a new MP3 player, new clothes, an upgrade on my video software, a car. My Shimas were getting pretty worn. I wondered if it would be so bad to try the Octanes.

One day after school, I skated past the Stairs and Sister Jude called out to me. She opened the gate and motioned me up the steps. I glanced down at my skates but she didn't seem to care so I clomped up and sat next to her.

"Tell me," she said. "Tell me everything and don't leave things out or change them just to make yourself look good." She lit a cigarette. "I hate that."

I knew she'd heard some of what had happened from my mom but I needed her to hear my side of the story. As I told her about the skate contest and the bridge, leaving out nothing,

I wondered if this was what going to confession was like. It was probably better than that because Sister Jude didn't try to be so superior around me anymore. She treated me like one of the bums.

"So I feel really bad," I explained. "They wouldn't let Corinne win because she was a girl. I was the only one who could have done something about it and I did nothing."

Sister Jude stared at me, then exhaled. "You usually get more than one opportunity to do the right thing. God has to give us lots of opportunities because we're so . . ." She took a drag off her cigarette, then savored it for a moment. "Human," she finished.

As she said this, it occurred to me what she thought I was supposed to do: cash the check and give the money to Loaves and Fishes. But that meant I'd be sponsored by Octane. Was doing the right thing with strings attached still doing the right thing? I remembered Paul Wellstone telling me that if he opposed the Iraq War, he could lose the election and all the good he could do. Then he voted against it anyway. "Thanks," I told Sister Jude and pushed past her to the big doors of the sanctuary. "You've been a big help."

She was so surprised she didn't even tell me to take off my skates. I ran into Billy on my way out. He was halfheartedly pushing a broom down the dimly lit hall, rearranging the dust bunnies. "I like your skates," he said, because he liked it that I was breaking the rules.

"Yeah, well they're mine," I joked. "You can't have them." I could have my dad help me work on them. I didn't really need those Octanes.

When I got home I dug through the laundry until I found the check in a pocket of my dirty jeans. I finally felt confident enough to get rid of it. As I turned on Dad's shredder, Lily walked in. "What're you doing?" she asked in her nosy little girl way.

"None of your business," I said, but I turned off the shredder.

"That's your check. Wait, I know what to do with it." She grabbed a metallic paint marker from Dad's desk and before I could stop her, grabbed the check and started drawing stars all over it.

"Lily!" I couldn't believe even she would do something like that. It was one thing if I wanted to wreck my check. I had kind of won it after all.

"Wait." She disappeared into my room, then came back with a book in one hand, the check in the other. "Bookmark." She tucked the check in Paul Wellstone's book.

I stared at her. "Lily, you're brilliant."

She looked surprised, then smiled. "Really?"

"Really."

On the last day of school, I hung around after Mr. Mac's class. We wouldn't find out how we did on the AP test until mid summer but I thought I had passed. I wanted to thank him for that.

Mr. Mac said to Corinne as she walked out, "I'll see you at the 11:00 summer school meeting, Ms. Camden." Corinne probably had to go to summer school so she didn't flunk. She wasn't doing so well in that class before losing the skate comp and afterwards she didn't seem to care.

"Mr. Snow?" Mr. Mac was wearing an AC/DC T-shirt instead of his usual button-down shirt and tie, which made the formalities coming out of his mouth sound a little surreal.

"I just wanted to thank you for being such a good teacher," I blurted out as he looked up in surprise from the piles of papers he was sorting. "Derrick and I decided we're going to do another History Day project together next year," I continued, embarrassed that I sounded like such a suck-up. We had made it to state that year and Derrick had decided that, with our two superior brains sparking as we butted heads, next year we had a chance at nationals. "Not that we're friends or anything."

"Really?" Mr. Mac grinned. "Maybe I'm a good teacher after all."

"Mr. Mac?" I said. "When you meet with Corinne could you tell her she's a good teacher too? I'd tell her myself but she's not talking to me."

"Corinne Camden?" Mr. Mac looked confused.

"Skating," I explained. "She's an awesome skating teacher."

"Skating?" His electric hair stood on end as he ran his fingers through it and I could tell he was filing this bit of information away in his teacher's bag of tricks.

"Have a good summer Mr. Snow." Mr. Mac turned back to his desk as the bell rang. "And carry it forward."

"Uh, yeah," I said. Carry it what?

"Like the Wellstone signs," he called after me. "You're a Wellstone supporter. Right?"

"Yes, sir," I said. I looked back at Paul Wellstone's name, faint but still legible at the top of the white board.

***

Saying goodbye to Lark was one of the hardest things I'd ever done. I wondered if I'd ever see her again and if I did if we'd still know each other. I didn't plan anything for this last night mostly because I didn't want it to happen. Now it seemed that once again I'd made her a low priority when that wasn't it at all. "Want to go to a movie?" I asked.

"Not really." Lark just sat there fingering the silk scarf she had looped around her throat like a little kid touching her security blanket.

"I got a present for you."

"Oh." Her face brightened.

"I'll go get it." I ran up the stairs to my bedroom. I stood for a second on the landing when I came back. I watched her on the couch, reapplying her lipstick like she always did, and I wished we could just hang out on the couch all night. I wished I could rewind the whole year, put it in the bail section and start over again.

I handed her the box I had wrapped in some paper I got from my mom. It was pretty and sort of perfumed like Lark. "It's not beautiful jewelry or anything."

She shrugged. "That's okay."

"I thought about getting you beautiful jewelry but . . ."

"That's okay."

"I wanted to get you something that would remind you of me, of your year here." She'd probably think I was cheap when actually it cost me a ton of money. All of the money I had started saving to replace my skates.

"Oh." She pulled it out and cupped it in the palm of her hand. It was a silver peace symbol on a chain. It wasn't girly or beautiful. It was cool. "You got this for me?" She hugged me and covered my face with kisses.

"Hey, watch the lipstick." I put up my arms to protect myself.

"Let's go for a walk," I said.

"A walk?" She didn't sound convinced.

"To the river," I said. The place I'd been afraid to return to since that night on the bridge. "The M-I-S-S-I-S-S-I-P-P-I."

"What?" Lark laughed.

"That's what little kids like Lily call it."

"M-I-S- what's the rest?" She wanted to memorize it, to bring the Mississippi and all of it back with her.

By the time we reached the river, it was turning dark and the streetlights were lighting our way. I thought how weird it was walking by one of the major rivers on earth with this girl from half a world away. We wound our way to the railroad bridge and sat on the concrete, my arm around her, her head on my shoulder. "When I visit you in Belgium, will you take me to walk by the river there?" I asked.

"No," she said. "I'll take you to the sea. It's big and cold and endless. It swallows up everything."

"Sounds scary." We both looked at the river and I remembered being out on that bridge and inching back to safety. I wrote in the journal I had to keep for Psychology about losing Oops. I wrote, "The river just took him away from us. There was nothing we could do but watch." Now Lark was going away. We sat and silently watched the restless water.

"What will you miss most about me?" Lark turned her face to mine.

"Your lipstick," I said, without thinking.

"Right." Her chocolatey smooth European voice sharpened with skepticism.

"I like watching you put it on. Even though you always do it at the worst time possible." She started to protest, but I went on. "I like it because it frames these amazing things that come out of your mouth. And even though I hate it, I like how it comes off on me."

She dug in her pocket for her ever-present tube of lipstick, put it on, then held my head as she pressed her lips against my cheek. "There, promise me you'll never wash it off."

"I promise," I said, holding my crossed fingers in front of her.

***

Camp Chickey Monkey was even worse than I expected. My parents invited Andy to come with us, which was incredibly awkward. He got in the car with his headphones on and didn't even acknowledge me. My mom took me aside when we got gas and pleaded with me, "Talk to him."

"No way," I said. "I didn't invite him."

So my parents tried to make small talk with Andy, which was very small, miniscule, consisting of their boring questions and his one-word answers. Even Lily fell asleep instead of bothering to listen. Even Yellow groaned in boredom.

The next day Andy and I sat by the lake, halfheartedly tossing a ball to Yellow, drinking cherry cokes and eating a bag of chips I'd ripped off from the kitchen. I couldn't take much more of his silent treatment, so I decided to be nice to him. I talked like he might be listening, bouncing the conversational ball off the wall between us.

"Great food," Andy said, finally giving into the pleasures of junking out and basking in the sun. "It's been a long time since I've snorted coke."

"What?" I said, snorting coke myself as I choked midstream and the bubbles backed up my nose.

Andy laughed at me. It was like we were in middle school again. The kind of dumb joke only a parent could hate.

"Let's see if we can get some dessert." I let Yellow stick his snout in the empty chip bag. We headed to the kitchen, where my female relatives were making all this food and not allowing anyone to eat it. There were rows of chocolate chip cookies cooling on the counter. I grabbed one and my aunt swatted my hand so the cookie hit the floor and crumbled.

"Out," she ordered. "Before you waste any more."

I swept the pieces into my hand, while Yellow snarfed up the crumbs. "Not wasted."

"Gene," Mom warned. "Behave."

"He's on a diabetic diet," Andy informed them. "He's trying to get diabetes," he explained, as I swiped another cookie.

All of the old ladies gasped at that, even though they were the ones who'd poured half a ton of sugar into the food they'd made for that night's dinner. Andy laughed.

"Here," I handed him the cookie as we got booted out.

After our Snow family mega feast, the adults poured wine from big jugs and popped open cans of Pig's Eye. One of the cousins from North Dakota, who worked as a DJ, played lame music in the pine-paneled dining hall where they moved the tables to create a dance floor. Andy and I sat on folding chairs, watching little kids like Lily run in circles to bad AM radio hits from the seventies. My aunts and mom sang along and danced to this putrid song "I Am Woman Hear Me Roar."

"We gotta get out of here," I told Andy, as some old people started slow dancing to "Taking Care of Business" by Bachman Turner Overdrive. I knew if he got really bored, Andy would start dancing too, to make fun of them. That would've been funny but, for some reason, I felt like letting all my relatives make idiots of themselves in peace. Just call me a peace activist.

We walked out to the fire pit where my dad and his brother were arguing about politics, their faces lit by the flames. This was entertaining because as far as I could tell, both of them were trying to convince each other of the same thing. They both insisted the other one had to support Howard Dean for president.

"What if he doesn't win?" Andy thought he was just making conversation.

They both stopped mid rant and turned their intensity on Andy. "He has to win," they said simultaneously. They finally noticed they were in total agreement and clinked their cans of Pigs Eye together.

"With your help we can win," I heard Paul Wellstone telling me. Okay, I thought, I'm helping, it just might take a little longer than we originally planned.

My mom and Lily joined us. "Have you seen the stars?" Lily asked. "There's shooting stars everywhere. The sky is full of wishes."

"Yeah, right," I said. "And you are full of—"

"Gene!" Mom said.

"There's supposed to be a meteor shower tonight," my uncle remembered. Then he and Dad started discussing astrophysics, shifting their competition from politics to science.

"We should check out the show," my uncle said, remembering there was some reality behind all their scientific theory. We stood and dutifully looked up. The sky was pulsing with shooting stars.

"Wow," Dad said. Then he and my uncle were silent.

"I have to go to bed," Mom announced.

"She drank too much wine," Lily pointed out.

Mom winced in anticipation of the blinding headache she'd have the next day. "I would like you to note I am not driving a car in this condition."

"Or falling off a bridge," added Andy.

"Oh, Andrew Carlson, that is so awful." Mom put her arm around him.

"Yeah, it was," Andy agreed. "It would have been worse if Gene wasn't there." I looked at him in surprise.

"Time for certain people to go to bed." Dad turned to Lily.

"Not me," Lily piped up.

"Yes you," Dad said. "We have a big day ahead of us tomorrow. We're going to the crash site." We were right by the place where Paul Wellstone's plane crashed. I expected to be creeped out by this but it was beautiful there.

"To bed," Dad ordered.

"Squirt," I mouthed. I wasn't going to bed for hours.

"I'll help you to the cabin," my uncle offered. He picked up my mom and started walking as she was flailing and laughing.

"I'll take Andy," Lily put her arms around him and actually boosted him off the ground.

"Hey." Andy pulled her up on his shoulders. "What are you—some kind of bionic babe?"

I stared at him as he walked off, my sister kicking him like she was digging spurs into a horse. Bionic babe was what he used to call Corinne.

Dad and I sat by the fire where he added another log and I poked it with a stick. Just like all the campfires we'd had since I was little.

"Dad?"

"What?" He was preoccupied with getting the wood just right so it would burst into flame.

It felt like such a magic day, a magical night. It felt like if I could just think of the right question, he'd give me the right answer that would make sense of everything.

"What kiddo?" he repeated, settling back on his log perch.

"Oh, nothing," I said, and it occurred to me that maybe life wasn't a multiple choice test after all. Maybe you were supposed to organize your life into an essay, support your thesis and wrap it all up with a good conclusion. But that didn't seem right either. In fact, that sounded really boring. Maybe life was just random like Andy's sense of humor and the answer was in the stories you made of it.

Dad looked up. "You can even see the stars from here."

"Yeah, it's like this weird cosmic energy." I followed his eyes. "I can feel them buzzing."

Dad went off on one of his tangents, another lecture about physics which was fascinating—to him at least. I half listened. Then suddenly he stopped. "You're right," he said. "I can feel them too."

We sat by the fire just taking it all in. The sky was alive and moving. It was like all the stars were on skates, streaking across it. The stars streaked electric around us, inside us. It felt like I was the one shooting through the sky, like buzz of pure light, sailing over the world on my skates. Like Airman. A falling star, unafraid of falling.

ACKNOWLEDGEMENTS

I am grateful to Joan Drury and Norcroft for giving me the time and space to begin and to the community of writers at the Loft for sustaining me. Much thanks to the good people at North Star Press for their dedication to bringing this and other beautiful books into the world.

This book would not exist without the deep attention and unwavering support of my writing group: Jeanne Farrar, Duke Klassen, Tyone LaDouceur, Kathy Lewis, Jane Lund, Kathy Ogle, and Danielle Sosin. It was helped along the way by these readers: Siana Goodwin, Christian Lauer, Sam Orfield and Jeanne Stuart. Thank you to my writing friend Jenny Hill, who sat across from me in coffee shops each week silently writing, and to Christine Murphey, for our enduring long-distance writing friendship.

My appreciation to Pam Costain for her thoughtful feedback about the Wellstone campaign. Any error in fact or tone is solely mine. I am indebted to Mary Logue for her insights into improving the book's structure. And thanks to Andy Snow for the use of his totally cool nickname.

Enormous gratitude to my writing teacher, Pat Francisco. Truly, this book could not have been written without you. Thank you for opening the door to the writing life and ushering me in.

Much love and thanks to my family: Rachel Kaspari, insightful first reader, my Lily; James Kaspari for lending me the details of his teenage life and generously giving me help and feedback when they became Gene's. Thank you, Jamie, for showing me the beauty, the athleticism, the total coolness of street skating and answering my endless questions. And finally, thanks to Brad Kaspari for his patience, his never-ending support and his ability to make supper magically appear on the table. Thank you, my best friend—for everything.

Pat Rhoades is a clinical social worker and writer who lives with her husband in Minneapolis next to the mighty Mississippi. *Rodeo Snow* is her first novel. You can visit Pat at patrhoades.com.